FOREVER MY GIRL

THE BEAUMONT SERIES

HEIDI MCLAUGHLIN

The song Painkillers provided exclusively by Eric Heatherly.
Flower Mound, TX

Edited by Fallon Clark
Cover Designed by: Letitia Hasser @ RBA Designs

❀ Created with Vellum

Dear Reader,

This cover is the movie tie-in version only. The content has not been changed to coincide with the movie.

The movie stars Alex Roe & Jessica Rothe with the screenplay written and directed by Bethany Ashton-Wolf.

FOREVER MY GIRL

For Madison & Kassidy

A light snore reminds me that I'm not alone. The heaviness of a body sprawled out, sets me off immediately. The stale smell of day old perfume lingers in the air and on my sheets.

The curtains are pulled back, the sun shining through the large window which affords me the best view and privacy.

Rolling over, there's a face I don't remember. A face that holds no name in my recollection or any vivid memory of how she ended up in my hotel room let alone my bed.

The bed part I can probably figure out.

The blonde hair tells me that I didn't bother to get her name or ask her what her favorite drink was. Guaranteed our conversation was eyes, hands and lips only. There is one hair color that can make my heart beat and blonde isn't it.

Neither is red.

Eyes too.

Never blue.

They have to be brown or green, never blue.

This isn't a downward spiral or some drug induced

moment. I don't do drugs, never have, but I may drink excessively on occasions like last night. This is me coping with my mistakes and failures. I may be successful when I'm on stage, but at night I'm alone.

And so freaking scared of dying alone.

I reach for my phone to check the time. Instead I pull up the gallery that holds her image, my thumb hovering over her face. I'll see her when I go home and I don't know what I'll say.

I know she hates me.

I hate me.

I ruined her life. That is what her voice message said. The one I've saved for the past ten years. The one I've transferred from phone to phone just so I could hear her voice when I'm at my lowest. I can recite every hateful word she said to me when I was too busy to answer and never found the time to call her back.

Never found one second to call and explain to her what I had done to us. She was my best friend and I let her slip through my fingers just to save myself from the heartache of hearing she didn't want me anymore.

I had dreams too.

And my dreams included her, but she would never have gone for it. I'm not living her American Dream. I'm living my own.

My decision destroyed everything.

My nameless bed cohabitant reaches out and strokes my arm. I move away quickly. Now that I'm sober, I have no desire to be anything to this person.

"Liam," she says through her seductive tone that sounds like a baby. It makes my skin crawl when women talk like this. Don't they see that it makes them sound ridiculous? No man worth his nuts likes this sort of thing. It's not sexy.

Wrapping the sheet around my waist I sit up and swing my legs over the edge, away from her and her wandering hand. My back tenses when I feel the bed shift. Standing, I pull the sheet tighter to keep myself somewhat covered. I shouldn't care, but I do. She's seen me in the dark, but I'm not affording her or her camera another look.

"I'm busy." My voice is strict, a well-practiced monotone. "Jorge, the concierge, will make sure you get a cab home."

I sleep purposefully facing the bathroom so I never have to look at them when I tell them to leave. It's easier that way, no emotions. I don't have to look at their faces and see the hope fade. Each one hopes they will be the one to tame me, to make me commit.

I haven't had a steady girlfriend since I entered the industry and a one night stand isn't about to change that. These girls don't mean anything and never will. I could change. I could settle down and marry.

Have a kid or two.

But why?

My manager, Sam, would love it, especially if it was her. She's my only repeat lay. The first time was an error in judgment, a lonely night on the road mistake. Now she wants more. I don't.

When she told me she was pregnant I wanted to jump off a cliff. I didn't want kids, at least not with her. When I think about having a wife, she's tall and brunette. She's toned from years of cheerleading and her daily five-mile run. She's not a power hungry executive in the music industry who spoke of hiring nannies before a doctor could confirm her pregnancy.

She suggested marriage; I freaked and flew to Australia to learn to surf.

She miscarried two months in. I made a vow that we'd keep things professional from that point on and that is when I started my one night stand routine. Despite everything, she still loves me, and is waiting for me to change my mind.

"You know," the barfly from last night starts to say in between shuffling and her huffed breathing as she puts on her clothes. "I heard you were a dick, but I didn't believe it. I thought we had something special."

I laugh and shake my head. I've heard it all, each one thinks we have something special because of the most amazing night they've ever had.

"I didn't pick you for your brains." I walk into the bathroom and shut the door, locking it for good measure.

Leaning against the door I bang my head against the solid wood. Each time I tell myself I'm going to stop, and I think I have until something makes me want to forget. My hands rake over my face in pure frustration.

I'm not looking forward to going home.

The reason for returning is staring at me from my bathroom counter. The page-long article of the guy I used to call my best friend. Picking up the paper, I read over the words that I have memorized.

Mason Powell, father of two, was killed tragically when the car he was driving was rear-ended by an eighteen wheeler.

Dead.

Gone.

And I wasn't there.

I left like a coward when I didn't say goodbye.

I changed my cell phone number because she wouldn't stop calling. I had to make a clean break and Mason was part of that. She and Katelyn were best friends and he'd tell her where I was and what I was doing. It was better this way.

I was only meant to be gone a year. I told myself I'd return home after twelve months, make everything right and show her that I wasn't the same person she fell in love with. She'd see that and thank me, move on and marry a yuppie business man, one who wakes up every day and puts on a crisp dress shirt and pleated slacks that she'd iron in their Leave it to Beaver household.

I squeeze the paper in my hands and think about everything I've missed. I don't regret it, I can't. I did this for me and did it the only way I knew how. I just didn't think I'd care so much about missing everything.

I missed the day he asked Katelyn to marry him. Something I knew he wanted to do since we were sixteen.

I missed his wedding and the birth of his twins. He was a father and a husband. He had three people who depended on him and now he's gone. He'll never see his children grow up and do the things that we did when we were younger. All the things we said our kids would do together. I missed this because I had something to prove to myself. I gave up on their dream and the life we had all planned out.

And now I'm heading home to face the music.

2

JOSIE

The words become a blur the longer I stare at them. The paper wet from my tears. Tears that haven't stopped falling since I received the phone call. Now I'm holding an order form with his name on it. The casket spray to be done in our high school colors – red and gold. The standing spray to be done in their wedding colors, our college colors, green and white. This is what Katelyn wants.

Katelyn is going to bury her husband in a few short days and yet she's sound enough to make decisions on what kind of flowers are going to drape over her husband's coffin.

Me? I can't even make it through reading the order form.

When Katelyn called and asked me to do the flowers it took everything in me to say yes when I really wanted to say no. I don't want to do this. I don't even want to believe that Mason is gone. I've known him since first grade and now he's gone. He won't be stopping in on Monday for his usual pick-up. Katelyn won't be getting her weekly dozen of roses, something she's been getting since he started proposing at seventeen.

They were the lucky ones, having it all figured out in high school and sticking with it. I thought I had that too, but I was blindsided my first semester in college. My life was turned upside down with just a few short words and a door slam, creating a wall between me and the love of my life.

I stand on shaky legs, wipe away my tears and make my way over to the door to flip the Closed sign to Open. I don't want to open today, but I have to. There is a wedding, homecoming and Mason's funeral in the next few days and I'm the lucky one doing all their flowers.

I pin Katelyn's order on the board next to the rest of the orders. I have to treat her like any other customer even though this is one I wish I wasn't filling.

Deep breaths, I tell myself as I start the first order. There are forty corsages and boutonniere's to make today and all I want to do is smash the roses between my palms and throw them out the door.

Door chimes break my concentration. Time to put on a happy face. Jenna is walking toward me, coffee cups in hand. I wipe my hands on my green apron and meet her at the counter.

"Thank you," I say just before sipping the hot liquid. The way to my heart is definitely through a caramel latte.

"I knew you needed it. I could sense your deep desire when I was in line."

Jenna is my part-timer and all over friend. She moved to Beaumont three years ago to escape an abusive husband and fit in instantly with me and Katelyn.

"How are you holding up?" she asks. I shrug, not really wanting to talk about things right now. I need to get through the day. As word starts to spread old classmates will be coming back and, as vain as it sounds, I want to look good. I don't want to look like I just got dumped because that is what most of them remember anyway.

"I just..." I hide my eyes behind my hand. "I don't have memories that don't involve Mason. I don't know what's going to happen on Monday when I open and he's not here to buy Katelyn's flowers. He's done that for over ten years."

"I'm so sorry, Josie. I wish there was something I could do for you guys."

"Just being there for Katelyn is enough. I'll handle my own feelings."

Jenna comes around the counter and gives me a hug before going to put on her apron. I'm thankful for her help, especially today. Maybe I can pawn off the funeral arrangements and focus on the happy.

But then again, maybe not.

Standing out front, staring into the shop is Mr. Powell. He looks lost. "I'll be right back," I say to Jenna as I slip out the door. The weather is breezy with a chill in the air. Definitely not your average Fall day here.

"Mr. Powell," I say, reaching out to touch his arm. He lost his wife last year to cancer and now his son – I can't imagine.

"Josephine." His voice is broken, horse. His eyes are hollow and bloodshot. "I was just walking and when I looked into the window here I remembered the first time I had to take Mason to get flowers for Katie. They were going to some dance and I was going to drive them." He shakes his head as if he's not sure if he's making it up or if he doesn't want to remember anymore.

"That was a long time ago, Mr. Powell. Do you want to

come inside and I'll call Katelyn for you? Maybe she can come pick you up."

He shakes his head. "I don't want to bother Katie. She has enough to worry about than to babysit her father-in-law." He stops speaking suddenly, his eyes glaze over. I look around to see what, if anything has caught his attention. "Am I still her father-in-law?"

My hand covers my mouth but it can't muffle my cry. "Of course you are," I whisper. "She's your Katie, you're the only one who gets to call her that, ya know. She loves you as if you're her own father."

Mr. Powell looks at me and nods before walking off. I want to follow him and make sure he makes it home or wherever he decides to go, but I stand frozen on the sidewalk watching him walk away.

Mason will never know the impact he's had on everyone in Beaumont.

When I make it back into the shop, Jenna is pulling the roses for the funeral sprays. I breathe a sigh of relief that I didn't have to ask her. She just knew. I walk up behind her and wrap my arms around her, hugging her, thanking her for being a good friend.

Orders come in like crazy, most of them for Katelyn or for the service. I keep my delivery boy busy today and each time he walks in he's smiling from ear to ear. I can't imagine why. Most people don't tip when they receive flowers for a funeral, unless of course, you're Mrs. Bishop, Katelyn's plastic stuck-up mom who is everything that the word 'proper' stands for.

Jenna and I work side by side. I try not to pay attention, but can't help but look over every few minutes. The arrangements are turning out beautifully. I'd like to think that Mason would be impressed.

"When are you going to say yes to Nick?"

I threaten to stab Jenna with my shears. "He asked again the other night," I say as I pull some baby's breath to cut.

"What number is that?"

I shrug. "I lost count."

Jenna tosses down her shears and places her hands on her hips. "What the hell are you waiting for? He has a good job, he loves you and he takes care of Noah. Not too many men want to play daddy when it's not their kid."

I try to hide my smile, but she punches me in the arm. "You said yes?"

I nod which causes her to jump up and down. She pulls my hand forward and frowns when she sees I'm not wearing a ring. "We're going wait until everything calms down. It's not time to celebrate, ya know? We both lost our friend and even though we're happy and in love, Katelyn and the kids mean more to us than telling everyone that we're finally getting married."

Jenna wraps her arms around me, holding me tight. "He'll make you happy, Josie."

"He already does," I reply when she steps back. I can already see the wheels turning in her head and this just solidifies what I said to Nick; we need to elope.

She turns back and starts working again. "Do you think he'll adopt Noah?"

I drop my shears onto the ground, barely missing my foot. I clear my throat. "I... I'm not sure about that."

"Why not? He's been raising him since he was what, three?"

I bite my lip and just nod at her. "We've never discussed it and I really don't want to talk about Noah's dad right now."

She looks at me and smiles. "Okay," she says, but I know she'll ask again.

I haven't thought about Noah's dad in years. No, that's not true. More like hours and even more so since Mason died. I don't know if he knows about Mason or even cares. I just hope he doesn't show up here.

3

LIAM

I rode at night to avoid people following me. I slept during the day and made it home in seventy-two hours.

Home.

What a strange word. For as long as I can remember, I've lived in a hotel. They're easy, peaceful with top notch security. I never have to leave if I don't want to. I have someone that does my grocery shopping and laundry. When something breaks, someone's there to fix it and my guests are screened.

The weather is colder than I remember. I hope my maid packed me the appropriate clothes. Sam is having a new suit sent to my hotel. She wanted to come with me for moral support, but I declined. I don't need her. I don't want her here. Just in and out I told her. Except I left a few days earlier than scheduled because I need time to see her.

Even if it's just to look at her from across the street, I need the extra time to remind myself why I gave up college and her dreams to spend countless days in a cramped studio and sleepless nights traveling in a bus across the country. I need the vision of her to drive the point home that I made the right decision for me, regardless of how much I hurt her.

I need to know if she's moved on, I hope that she has. How many kids does she have and what does her husband do for a living? I only hope he treats her better than I ever did because she deserves it and so much more.

Pulling into the Holiday Inn just outside of Beaumont, I shut off my bike before the manager comes out to tell me I'm disturbing the peace. With the kickstand down and my helmet off, I slip on a pair of fake eyeglasses and pull a baseball cap down low. I know word will spread once I step foot into Beaumont, but for a few days I'd like to be anonymous. I slide my arms into my weather proof guitar case and unhook my bag from the back of my bike.

The walk to the lobby is painstakingly long. This hotel isn't far off the highway and the noise is very present. This is the most unassuming hotel and one people wouldn't think to look for me. I remember when I told Sam to book my room here I thought I killed her with just the words of a three star Notel Motel. Yet here I am walking into a commoner lobby with the TV blaring and stale coffee sitting in the pot next to this morning's donuts.

"How can I help you?" The clerk is speaking even before I'm in the door. Her voice is high-pitched and annoying; a sharp and painful reminder of nails across the blackboard. Her hair is pulled back so tight that her face has no option but to smile. Her lips are painted Hollywood red. I want to hand her a Kleenex and tell her that guys in Hollywood really don't go for the whole lipstick thing because it's evidence.

But I don't. I don't say hi or even smile at her. I just want to get to my room and maybe sleep a little. "I need to check in," I tell her. I hand her my driver's license and wait.

My fingers start tapping on the counter as she types my name into the computer. Each time she looks up at me and smiles, I want to step back. Someone ought to tell her that she wears too much make-up and if she pulls her hair any tighter she'll be bald.

"Is Mr. Westbury your dad? He's the professor for my poli-sci class," she asks with a hopeful gleam in her eye. I shake my head no even though the answer is probably yes. I wouldn't know since he hasn't spoken to me since I dropped out of college.

"Oh, well that's too bad. He's a really great professor."

"Lucky you," I say. Her face deadpans at my lack of enthusiasm.

"If there's anything I can do for you just let me know," she says back in her high-pitched annoying and very childish voice. She sets the keycards down on the counter and asks me to fill out the car registration slip. I write down only the pertinent information, avoiding the make and model of my bike. They don't need to know.

I pick up the key cards and head to the elevator. When I step in, I look at the card and sigh. I'm on the sixth floor, the highest one they have, but not high enough for me. This will have to do and it's only short term. I'm just here to say goodbye to Mason and stare at her for a bit before returning to my life.

The hallway reeks. That is the first thing I notice when I step out of the elevator. That and the ugly ass carpet lining the halls. I despise the smell of stale smoke. I push into my room, dropping my bag onto one of the double beds. I walk over to the sliding glass door, throw open the thick dark curtains and stare out at the lights of Beaumont. I flick the latch and open the door, stepping out into the chilled air.

The sound of breaking glass causes me to look left.

Immediately, I wish I hadn't because just off in the distance is the water tower Mason and I, along with a few others, used to climb after our games. We'd take a case of beer up there, leave the girls down at the bottom and see who could hit the bed of my truck with their empty bottles.

"Looks like someone is carrying on our tradition," I say to no one.

"Mase, come down here. I'm lonely," Katelyn yells up at him.

The laughter between us and the girls is just enough to keep a constant flow of noise in the air.

"I love you baby," Mason yells through cupped hands.

"I'm going to marry that girl and make beautiful babies with her." We start laughing, but I know it's true. Katelyn walks on water where Mason is concerned. I know the feeling. I look down and see the silhouette of my girl standing by my truck, my letterman jacket making me jealous because it's wrapped around her. But this is tradition.

"I know man," I say, patting him on the back.

"Double wedding," he shouts as I spew my beer out into the open air.

"Dude, you're a dude. You aren't supposed to talking about weddin's and shit." Jerad says before chugging his beer.

Mason shrugs. "When you love someone, you just know."

Nothing is the same and everything could've been just like it was planned out. Mason's not supposed to be gone. If anything, it should be me. I screwed up the plan.

I step back into the room, closing the door and pulling the curtains closed. When I look at the bed, it's mocking me, telling me I'm uninvited. It doesn't want me as much as I don't want it.

I can't stay here. This room is going to suffocate me. I

get rid of my disguise and grab my jacket and helmet. Maybe riding will clear my head, but then again, maybe not. The last time I went on an unplanned road trip I made a life-altering decision.

The red exit sign above the staircase is more inviting than the elevator. I slam my shoulder into the door and rush down the stairs, sliding down the railing just like I did when I was younger, something I haven't done in a long time.

My helmet is on before I reach the lobby. The last thing I want is the receptionist tart getting any ideas about who I am. My luck, she'd let herself into my room, lie on the bug infested bedspread and wait for me to claim her.

I'll pass.

"Do you need a wake-up call?" she asks as I rush through the lobby. Is she serious? I pull out my phone and look at the time, it's after midnight.

I shake my head. "I'm good," I say as I throw open the door and head for my bike.

There is nothing like the roar of an engine. The vibration alone comforts me. I spin the throttle before kicking my bike into gear and tear out of the parking lot. I can feel her watching me, I'd bet anything she's licking her lips with excitement.

With no destination in mind I stick to the back roads. The less traffic the better. Just me and the road and the looming sun threatening to rears its ugly head for yet another day of bullshit.

I'm shocked when I hit the Beaumont line. Well, not really. I've been thinking about this town non-stop since I learned about Mason. The town is quiet, wrought iron lights lighting the path through the streets.

Nothing has changed.

I slow down as I make my way through town. Turn left,

turn right and end up on the street I grew up on. When I stop in front of my childhood home, one light on outside and one on inside, I know my dad's awake.

Nothing has changed.

The two-story white house with the red door is the same. No cars in the driveway, lawn manicured to perfection. My room is dark and I wonder what they did with it. Are my pictures still lining the hallway or did those come down when I betrayed them in the worse way? What will they say when their defiant son knocks on the door and wants to stay for dinner?

I drive two blocks down and one over and stop in front of the Preston house. I'm not a fool to think she still lives here, but I know she wouldn't miss this unless she and Katelyn are no longer friends.

The porch light flips on and the door opens. Mr. Preston, the man who was to be my father-in-law, steps out onto the porch. I know he can't see me through my darkened helmet, but maybe he's wondering.

He stands there and stares at me and I at him. He's aged, just like I'm assuming my father has. He steps down onto the grass and that's my cue to go. I hit the throttle and take off down the street, leaving Mr. Preston in his yard wondering.

4
———

JOSIE

I pull into the driveway of Katelyn and Mason's modest ranch home, matching pink tricycles sitting in the yard. I can't bring myself to get out of the car. It's like accepting the inevitable. I know nothing will bring back Mason or change what has happened, but maybe I can prolong it just a little bit longer.

"Aunt Joey what are you doing?" I jump at the little voice that snuck up on me. Peyton is staring at me, standing by the passenger side of the car. Her dark curly hair is in pigtails tied with ribbons and her toothless grin lights my day.

"Nothing, sweetie, just thinking," I say as I get out of the car and walk around to where she's standing. She's in her Sunday football jersey and sweatpants and has a football tucked under her arm. She's every bit Mason.

"Where's Noah?"

"He's at school."

Her face falls as she looks down at the ground. Her little sneaker-clad foot starts swinging back and forth. "Mama says we don't have to go to school until after." Her voice trails off.

I fight back the tears as my heart breaks for her and her sister. They only got five years with their dad and will only remember one if they're lucky. I bend down in front of her and wipe a stray tear off her cheek. "Noah can come over after school before he goes to practice, okay?"

She nods and I bring her into my arms, carrying her into her once-happy home.

This is my first time in the Powell home since the night we got the call. I came over here to stay with the girls while Katelyn was in the hospital waiting for a sign that Mason was going to make it. I paced the floor, the same floor they paced when the girls had colds or the flu and kept them up at night.

The same floor that Mason dumped a plate full of chicken when he tripped over the bag of footballs he forgot to put away after practice. Katelyn and I laughed so hard. When he stood up Mason had chicken grease all over his face. One look from him and Katelyn knew he was coming after her.

I set Peyton down and kiss her on the forehead. I don't even know how to comfort her and her sister, let alone her mom.

"Where's your sister?" I ask.

Peyton shrugs. "With mama, I guess."

"Aunt Joey who is going to watch football with me now?" her voice breaks as she asks the simplest question of all.

Usually I have an answer for everything, but when I look into her eyes I don't know what to say to her because there isn't an answer. It could be me one week or Mr.

Powell, but it will never be Mason. He was her football buddy and she his.

"I'm sure Nick would love to and even Noah. Maybe your Grandpa can come over on Sundays."

"It's not the same," she whispers before leaving me in the middle of the room surrounded by nothing but memories, once in a lifetime moments captured by a real life lens and frozen in the past. And sometimes that's not enough. Any memories made now won't have Mason.

"Hey." I turn to find Katelyn behind me. Her hair is pulled back in a sloppy bun and she's wearing one of Mason's shirts. I can't hold back the tears and choke on a sob as I rush to hold her. She cries into my chest, her sobs shattering my reserve.

"I'm so sorry," I say softly to her. Her hands are clutching at my shirt as she fights to control herself. She was there for me when my world fell apart and I'm going to be there for her, even if it kills me.

When she pulls back I wipe her tears just like I did for Peyton. "You seemed okay yesterday," I say trying to remind her that she is having a few good moments.

"Yesterday I didn't have to make any decisions except what color flowers I wanted. Today I have to pick a casket and bring..." she takes a deep breath, covering her face with her hands. Her diamond engagement ring is sparkling as it catches the sunlight. "I have to pick out his last outfit and I don't know what he'd want to wear."

This is something I can't even imagine. I wouldn't know what to do. When things changed for me I wanted to die, but Katelyn and Mason held me together. They were my glue. The love of my life didn't die, he just decided I was no longer what he needed in life and went away. I didn't have to bury him or clean out his office. He took my heart with him when he shut the door.

"I think maybe you should ask the girls what they want him to wear. Let them help you because you are going to need them to get through all of this. I know Peyton is worried about who will watch football with her on Sunday."

"I know," she sighs heavily. "Elle wants to know who is going to tuck her in at night because no one does it like daddy."

I pull her back into my arms and hold my friend. There are no words that I can say that will solve this dilemma for her, only time will. But time hurts.

Katelyn takes my advice and asks the twins to help pick out their dads final outfit. When they come out, the three of them are holding a mismatch of clothes. Katelyn shows me a pair of dark slacks. Peyton holds up his coaching shirt and Elle shows me the shoes he'll be buried in, one cleat and one tennis shoe. I crack a smile which causes them all to laugh.

It's perfect and so very Mason.

The drive to the funeral home is quiet. Katelyn plays with her rings, much like she did when she got engaged. I look down at my bare hand, and wonder when Nick will slip a ring on my finger. There doesn't need to be an announcement; people expect it. Nick and I have been together for six years. It was time to make a decision. A man like Nick isn't going to wait around forever. Everyone says he's a catch because he's the one of us who really made something out of his education and they're right. I'd be stupid not to marry the town's pediatrician.

Picking out a casket is a lot harder than it seems. You can pick the type of wood, inlay and the color. All things that Katelyn had to decide while sitting in an office that smells like dead people.

Katelyn has to pick music, programs and list the pall bearers. I watch as she writes down the names, leaving the sixth spot blank.

"You forgot one," I point out.

She shakes her head. "Just in case," she says. She doesn't have to explain what she means, I know who she's referring to, but I don't want to think about... him.

After I drop her off, I head home. Noah should be back from school and I just want to hug him until I'm reasonably certain he's never going to leave me.

"Noah?" I call as I enter the house. The TV is on and I find him lying on the couch. He's watching an old game film of Mason and Nick from high school. I hear that familiar name and look down at Noah, running my fingers through his hair. "What's going on, buddy?"

"Just watching," he says, curling into my hand.

I sit down and cuddle him into my lap. I love that he is still my little boy when I need him to be.

"You look so funny, mom." He starts laughing. I pull his hair and pinch his ear just so I can continue to hear his giggles.

"Just wait until you're my age and we watch your videos."

"Anyone home?"

"In here," I yell as Nick comes into the house. He takes one look at what we're watching and scoots in behind me, wrapping his arm around my shoulders.

"Why are we watching this?" he whispers into my ear. I shrug and motion toward Noah. Nick knows I'd never put this in, watching these highlights does nothing but open old memories.

Noah continues to laugh at me and Nick about how funny we looked in high school. Each time I remind him that I have naked baby pictures of him and I'll be showing them to all his girlfriends.

Beaumont wins the game and that's my cue to turn it off. I search for the remote, panic setting in. I don't want to see what's at the end.

"Mom, who are you kissing?"

I look at the screen and see the boy that haunts my dreams and reality. He turns and faces the camera, his arm slung around me. When I see his blue eyes I bite my lip. I've been thinking about him more and more since Mason died, and I wonder if he's happy. I get up and turn off the TV so I don't have to look at him anymore.

"He's no one, baby." I say as I leave the room.

5

LIAM

Driving through town last night was a mistake. Stopping in front of the Preston house was an utter lapse in judgment. I was surprised to find that Mr. Preston was awake, let alone willing to come outside and stare down a stranger on a motorcycle, especially one dressed in all black.

The walls of this hotel room are closing in and fast. I should've stayed farther out of town where I could at least have a suite with space to move. I need to pace and think. Think about what I'm going to do when I see her. I just want to look. I need to know that she's okay and happy. That she's moved on with her life and I'm nothing but a blip on her radar.

Maybe she buys my music because she can say she once knew me, a long time ago. I've pictured her many times standing in the line at the grocery store holding People or Rolling Stone when I'm on the cover. I want to think that she's read the articles and seen me talk about her without actually saying her name. That she's created a playlist on her iPod of all the songs that are about her, that she knows I've never stopped loving her.

I pound my fists into my head. *"You're so stupid, Liam. She doesn't fucking care about you. You left her and changed your number so you wouldn't have to listen to her crying on your voicemail."*

I have to get out of this hotel because staying here just reminds me of her and the night we lost our virginity to each other and it's driving me insane.

With my helmet on before I reach the lobby, I sprint through the door avoiding the day clerk that is working. She's actually a bit cuter then the night clerk, but not by much. There's nothing worse than a woman who tries too hard.

I speed through the back roads, taking corners faster than I should, passing cars that are going too slow and blowing by a school bus full of kids. A few horns honk and windows roll down, hands flying out. I don't bother to look in my mirror to see them flipping the bird. I've done it before to whatever jackass thinks he owns these roads.

Mason and I used to own these roads. We were so stupid when we were younger. Always driving too fast or drinking, not to mention the many games of mailbox baseball. Hell, I used to make-out with my girl while driving, letting her straddle me just so I could feel her against me before dropping her off at home.

Hot summer nights spent in the back of my truck looking at the stars, holding her between my legs with my arms wrapped around her. I told her I'd love her forever. I said I love you first and promised to never let her go.

I pull up short and pull over into a parking lot. I need to calm down. Driving like an idiot doesn't solve anything. The last thing I want is my name in the paper because I was being reckless. I've worked hard to keep my image clean. No more mistakes for me.

When I look up I see that I'm at the Allenville Museum, a place dedicated to high school sports. I get off my bike and walk in, paying the five dollar admission. Inside it's like a shrine. I'm hanging from the ceiling with my record breaking stats displayed under my picture. There's a picture of Mason and I together. We were supposed to break records at the University of Texas but he wanted to stay close to Katelyn and opted to go to the state school with her. He was the smart one.

A large picture of Mason is front and center in the museum with a black cloth draped over the edges. There is a table next to his picture with more photographs from high school, with a few of him and me and some of the other guys. We're all so young in our football uniforms, holding up our index finger telling the world that we're number one. We didn't have a care in the world, we just wanted to win. One of our championship footballs sits on a stand. I want to touch it, feel the pigskin against my fingers, but I refrain. Those days are gone. I left them all behind when I packed up and left Texas for the bright lights of the big city.

"Do you hear that crowd?" Mason yells at me before we leave the tunnel. This is our last game ever in high school and this year we've gone undefeated. We annihilated the competition. Mason is so close to breaking the state record for rushing yards and I broke the record for passing earlier this season. We both signed our letters of intent for the University of Texas this morning.

And now we're about to play for our fourth state title.

"Yeah man, I hear it. Crazy, right?"

"There has to be more people than last year."

Of course there is. We are the best.

I slap my girl's ass as she passes by with her white, gold and red cheerleading skirt flipping up as she runs. She turns around and saunters up to me with that look in her eye. I know what she's expecting and I plan to deliver.

"You know how sexy I think you are when you bite your lip? You have this look in your eyes, Liam. Do you have plans for us later?" she whispers into my ear. My focus is now solely on her instead of the game as her hand sneaks under my t-shirt. There is nothing better than her skin against mine.

"Knock it off you two," Mason says as he slaps me in the back of the head. "If you give him a stiffy during the game, some linebacker is going to break his pecker."

We all start laughing. She kisses me goodbye, telling me to kick ass. She never wishes me good luck, just to kick ass.

I slip on my helmet and run out onto the field. We run through the cheerleaders and the student body. Music is blaring as we are announced onto the field. Parents and fans are on their feet in the stands, yelling loudly.

Mason and I go off to the side and warm-up, always together. We have a routine and we aren't about to break it now.

When the whistle blows, I take center with Mason on my left. The play is for him. He needs only one hundred yards to break the state record for rushing and I'm going to make sure that happens tonight. Our first play is a hand-off to him; he breaks the first tackle for a thirty yard gain.

We do this over and over until his dad holds up a sign showing 100 and I know. I hand Mason the ball and watch him jog it over to his dad. They hug and the fans go nuts. Mason Powell just set the state's all-time leading rushing record with nine thousand five hundred and two.

I remember that game as if it was yesterday and

standing here makes it feel like it was. I can almost smell the concession stand cooking hotdogs and popcorn. I can hear the cheers and feel the vibration from stomping feet on the bleachers.

I can still see Mr. Powell's face when Mason broke that record. I wanted my dad to look at me like that.

As I walk around I see us everywhere. The four state titles we won in football and two in baseball. Nick Ashford is staring back at me, his smug smile as he holds his most valuable player award. He wanted to be me. When he came to Beaumont he followed me around. He was always hanging out with us like he was our life-long friend, when all he wanted was my girl.

Other than Mason, I don't know what happened to any of my classmates. I didn't keep in touch because I had nothing to say and didn't want to hear what a failure I was for dropping out of college. I had to make the best choice for me and I did even though I know I hurt everyone that I loved, especially her.

When a group of young kids come pouring in I duck into the bathroom. I'm not expecting them to know who I am, but their teachers might and I don't want to sign autographs or pose for pictures. I just want to be me even if it's short-lived.

When I come out of the john there's a young boy standing at the counter with his hands under the water. I look at him through the mirror. He's crying even though he's trying to wash away the tears by splashing water on his face.

He's sort of small and his hair is a bit longer than normal for boys his age. Maybe he's being bullied and hiding in here. I hate bullies. Mason and I wouldn't stand for any bullying when we were in school. We made sure of it.

"You okay, bud?" I ask against my better judgment. I

don't want to know because I don't want the confrontation, but I can't stand seeing kids cry.

He nods and covers his face. "I'm not supposed to talk to strangers," he says. Smart kid.

"You're right. I just want to make sure you don't need your teacher or anything."

"No, I'm okay."

"Good deal." I wash my hands looking back at the boy through the mirror. He's watching my every move, eying the tattoos on my forearms, probably wondering if I'm going to kidnap him now that he's spoken to a stranger.

"Hey Mister, I know you."

I wipe my hands on the paper towel without giving much away. "You do, huh?" I say with no eye contact.

"Yeah, you're the one kissing my mom in the video I have."

I think back to my many music videos and don't remember kissing anyone. "Did you see this on TV?" I ask.

"No, you were in a football uniform."

I freeze. I've only ever kissed one girl while wearing a football uniform. I look at the boy, really look him over. His dark hair and elongated chin and his piercing blue eyes. It can't be.

There's no fucking way.

"Oh yeah, who's your mom?" I ask, playing it off.

"Josie Preston."

"Is that so?" I ask barely able to make the words come out of my mouth.

He nods and smiles real big showing some missing front teeth. "Did you kiss my mom a lot?"

What do I tell this boy? I can't exactly tell him the truth, especially not knowing what's going on. "Yeah, your mom was real beautiful. I bet she still is."

He nods in agreement. I used to think my mom was the prettiest until I couldn't stand to look her at her and watch her robotic ways.

"I gotta go. See ya around," he says. Before I have a chance to respond, he's out the door.

I run out of the restroom and museum as fast as I can. The boy tried to talk to me as I went by, but I ignored him. I need answers and whether I'm ready or not, she is going to give them to me.

I have to slow down when I hit Main Street. I can't afford someone getting suspicious or risk being pulled over. I park across from her shop and watch the door for a minute. I've known about the florist shop for a few years. When our anniversaries came up or I was homesick, I Googled her like a crazy stalker and found out what she was up to, but nothing I read said anything about a kid.

I drive around until its dark, waiting for closing. I don't want an audience. I pull up just as she steps out with a short red head. They hug goodbye and she looks at me. Her features are soft and she's not scared of this stranger on a motorcycle covered in black. She doesn't know who I am, she's just being friendly.

I have no game plan as I watch her step back inside. She switches the Open sign to Closed. If I'm going to do this, I need to do it now before she locks the door. Leaving my helmet on, I open the door, the bells alerting her to my presence.

"We're closing up," she says from somewhere in the shop. I can't see her, but I can feel her in the room.

I take off my helmet and pull off my gloves setting them on the counter. She doesn't see me when she comes around the corner.

"How old is he, Jojo?"

6

JOSIE

My hands fly to my mouth in a lame attempt to catch the gasp escaping. The vase I'm holding crashes to the floor, the water drenching my shoes, socks and jeans. I step around the broken glass and destroyed flowers for a better visual. I close my eyes before looking at the man standing at my counter.

It's him.

I can sense him; feel him moving across my skin like he's never left. When I open my eyes, he's staring at me. I remind myself that I need to be strong. I call the shots here.

"What are you doing here?" I barely squeak out. My voice is hoarse as if I've been yelling for hours on end. It's not strong and determined. It's not the authoritative voice I've practiced in the mirror a thousand times over for this moment.

He moves toward me. I step back and put up my hand. I don't want him to come any closer. He looks dejected. He puts his hands into his pockets and looks down. I don't want to look at him, but I can't help it. It's been ten years and he's changed so much, yet everything is the same in the way he looks at me.

"Jojo."

"Don't call me that," I blurt out.

"Why not? It's your name."

I shake my head, biting the inside of my cheek. I know why he's here and I want to hate Mason for it. I want to kick and scream and punch him for doing this to me... us. Everything was okay and now it's not.

He smirks and shakes his head, taking a step back and leaning against the counter. I break eye contact with him when he bites his bottom lip. I clear my throat and move away from the broken glass.

"What are you doing here, Liam?"

He shrugs. "Do you have something to tell me?"

I shake my head, bringing my hand to my forehead to push off the pending headache. This is not happening right now, it can't be. "No, we have nothing to talk about. You made that very clear that night in my dorm room."

Liam moves away from the counter, he stops at a few of the plants nearby, rubbing their leaves between his fingers before stalking toward me. I have nowhere to go. I could run, maybe scream and alert the neighboring business next door, but what good would that do? One look at Liam means their golden child is back in town. Everyone will be so happy.

"What's his name, Josie?" he asks bluntly as he get closer to me.

"Why do you care?" I fire back. His eyes throw daggers. I don't care if he's some hot shot musician. He left me. "You should go."

"Nah," he says shaking his head. He steps closer and I step back. I can't move anymore without falling into a display of flowers. He holds up his hands. "I just want to talk. I don't think you want me to start asking questions, do you?"

I shake my head no. Liam asking questions throughout town is the last thing I want. I don't want Noah's name brought up and people pointing fingers at him, even though some already do.

"How old is he, Jojo?" he asks in the same tone he would tell me that he loved me in when we'd walk from class to class or when he'd drop me off after a date.

"He'll be ten in June."

He steps back and looks at me. I can see the hurt in his eyes but I don't care. He left me. He left me to raise a baby on my own.

"What's his name?" the hurt evident in his voice, but I can't let that get to me. I can't. I need to be strong.

"Noah."

"When can I meet him?"

I laugh at his question and take this opportunity to move away from him. He stays where he is. I move behind the counter and start putting my things away. "You can't, there's no need."

"What the fuck do you mean I can't? I have a son. A son that you kept from me and you're telling me I can't meet him?"

"What makes you think he's yours?" I regret the words the moment they leave my mouth. Sheer pain washes over his face and I feel a small amount of elation for hurting him.

"You're telling me you cheated on me? Is that it, Jojo?" I don't have time to react before he's next to me. His cologne overcomes me, making my heart beat faster. Over the years I've wondered if he'd changed the Burberry cologne I bought him, but he hasn't and I have to fight every desire I have to reach out and touch him.

"I love you, Jojo," he whispers into my ear. He moves with fluidity and desire. I know I'm his first, I've never doubted that. I bury my head into the crook of his neck; he smells so good, desirable, and sexy. My body sings a song and only he has the melody.

I look into his eyes, his forehead rests upon mine. His mouth drops open when my fingers trail down his body, pushing him deeper.

"You're so perfect," he kisses me in between the words, showing me how much he loves me.

"I love you, Liam."

"You're forever my girl."

"Why are you flushed, Jojo?"

"Please stop calling me that," I all but beg. He steps away and leans on the other side of the counter.

"Sorry," he says. He starts playing with his lower lip and I want to slap his hand away and tell him to knock it off. "Did you cheat on me?"

I can't answer him. I don't want to answer him. Even if I did it's none of his business, but he knows me. He knows I didn't, he's just waiting for confirmation.

"You don't get to come in here and demand answers, Liam. You've been off playing rock star. You're the famous Liam Page. You left this," I spread my arms around and point to myself. "You left me. There's no room for you here."

He laughs. "That's not very hospitable of you. Whatever happened to the old adage that you can always go home?"

"People don't disappear without a freaking phone call or letter for ten years. People don't show up at your dorm and break up with the one they said they love and never return phone calls." I hide my face behind my hands. I didn't want this to happen. I could've gone twenty years and been okay without seeing him again. I fight to keep the tears away. I've shed enough tears over this boy to last a lifetime. I can't shed anymore.

"People change," he says.

"I don't want to do this with you."

"Right now?" he asks.

I shake my head. "No, never. I have nothing to say, Liam. You said what you had to that night and you didn't wait to hear what I had to say or answer any of my calls. I don't have to listen to your excuses and I definitely don't owe you anything."

I turn away so I don't have to look at him anymore. I need to stay strong and level-headed. I need to channel the breathing techniques that the doctor gave me before I had Noah.

"You expect me to walk away knowing I have a son?"

I snicker. "Yeah I expect you go walk out the door, get on your fancy bike, go back to your celebrity girlfriend and back to wherever it is you came from. There's nothing here for you and I don't want you hurting my son. I don't want him to know you just so you can walk away and out of his life for the next ten years." I wipe a tear that drops from my eye. I will not show him the effect he has one me.

"I don't have a girlfriend."

"Oh my god, Liam, from everything I just said you pick out the girlfriend part?" I shake my head. When I turn back around he's looking down at the ground.

"We've moved on and you're not part of our lives. Noah doesn't need you, he doesn't even know you so please just go and don't come back."

Liam nods his head. He doesn't make eye contact with me as he walks by. I watch his body, the same body that I know every inch of as it moves around my counter to where his helmet is resting.

"See you around, Josephine."

He's only called me Josephine one other time in my life, the night he broke up with me. Once the door closes and he's on his bike I break down. I fall to the ground, clutching my sides as I cry. Cry for ten years of missing him and him missing everything, including Noah.

"Hello," I growl into the phone, pissed that someone is waking me up before the sun has even decided to rear its ugly head today. I squint at the clock, its red numbers showing me that it's just after five in the morning. I'm supposed to be on vacation and I can't even sleep in.

"Rough night, Cowboy? I thought this was a get in and get out trip? According to my calculations, you left three days ago. It would seem you've decided to spend some extra time there. What's going on?"

"Jesus Christ, Sam it's like five o'clock. What the hell do you want?"

"Well," she pauses. I know she's looking at her finger nails, probably thinking she needs another manicure or something. I don't really care, I just want to sleep and forget yesterday ever happened. "When are you coming home?"

"Soon." I'm too exhausted to play her game. I should've fired her a long time ago, but I didn't and now I'm stuck.

"Liam," she says my name so softly I know what's coming. I'm in no mood to deal with her crap today.

"Not now, Sam."

"I miss you. It's been almost a week since we've seen each other. Let me come be there with you. You need me."

"No."

I hang up on her. I can't deal with her and I definitely don't want her here pretending we are more than what we are. My biggest mistake was sleeping with her. No, that's not true. My biggest mistake was leaving Josie in her dorm room that night and not dragging her with me. If I had we'd be married and parents. Maybe we'd have another baby by now.

Hell maybe we'd be divorced and nothing would be any different. She'd still hate me.

I climb out of bed slowly and make my way into the shower. After my encounter with Josie last night I came back here to leave my bike and walk to the nearest bar. Not being in Los Angeles cramps my style a bit. It's not like I can call someone to come pick me up and I knew I'd be too wasted to drive back last night.

I stand under the hot spray, allowing it to pulsate down on the top of my head. I think I've been dreading this day most of all. Secretly I was hoping it would never arrive, that my days would just replay themselves over and over again, like a music track I'm trying to dub.

I shut off the water once it turns cold and don't bother to dry off as I fall back onto the bed. I could strangle Sam for waking me up. I know she does it on purpose because she doesn't want me to forget she's there... in the background pushing for the title of *girlfriend*. She loves to accompany me on the red carpet. The thought that the press thinks we're a couple is thrilling to her. Sam wants the full package; the money, the fame and her face on every magazine and she thinks I'm the ticket. It doesn't matter how many times I've told her.

I don't want her.

I wake for the second time when the hotel phone rings. The front desk calls to tell me my suit is being brought up and that the rental car I ordered is waiting for me out front. I didn't think showing up to my buddy's funeral on my Ducati would be very appropriate.

I dress in my black pinstriped suit. Sam ordered three new dress shirts in basic colors, black, white and blue. I opt for white with a black tie, simple and sleek.

With one last look in the mirror I pocket my sunglasses. I may be known as Liam Page, but today I'm Liam Westbury and I'm going to mourn the passing of my friend.

The drive to the church is quick. I'm sitting in the parking lot contemplating my next step. I don't want to take the attention away from Katelyn so I'm trying to just sneak in right before it starts, then I'll be able to sneak out. I can pay my respects and say my peace at the cemetery before leaving town tomorrow.

When the last of the stragglers are in, I make my way toward the doors. Music plays from the inside, barely audible but it's an instrumental of our high school fight song. You'd think Mason planned this himself.

I pull open the heavy door and stand there until it shuts quietly. I walk over to the guest book and sign my name so that when Katelyn looks back she'll know I was here even if we didn't talk.

"I didn't think you'd show up."

I turn to see Katelyn standing behind me. She's wearing a knee length black dress with a black hat on. She doesn't look a day over eighteen.

"I have no excuses Katelyn. I just came to pay respects."

"I don't care –"

"I'll go. I'm not here to ruin your day. I'm very sorry for your loss." I return the pen to the pedestal and nod at her. Her hand on my arm halts my escape. She wants to yell at me and I deserve it. I deserve everything she and Josie want to throw at me.

"I'm a pallbearer short," she says, taking a deep breath. "I was hoping you'd show up, maybe a bit earlier than five minutes before the ceremony, but whatever. I'm not going to judge you, Liam. But I am going to ask you to walk Mason toward his final resting place and be by his side until he's safe again."

There are tears pooling in my eyes. I told myself I wouldn't cry, but I can't help it.

"I'd be honored." I manage to get out before losing it all. She nods and tells me to follow her. We walk through a door and a collective gasp falls over the room. I recognize a few guys from high school, but the one that stands out is Nick. He being here is shocking. They were never friends in high school. Guess life changes a lot over ten years.

Katelyn tells everyone on the left side to shift down one. "He'd want to be on your left." She places her hand on my face and leans in to kiss me on my cheek. Mason married a fine woman.

We receive our cue and heft Mason off the cart holding him up. When the vestibule doors open everyone turns. The hushed murmurs and finger pointing make me feel like I'm eating dinner in a crowded restaurant and they'll all be asking for my autograph the minute my plate is taken away.

With Mason in the center, his flowers draped over his casket, the other pall bearers take their seats. I watch as Nick sits down next to Josie and pulls her hand into his. I'm seeing nothing but red, she won't even look at me. But Noah waves at me and I wave back causing Nick's face to turn an ugly shade of green.

When I look down a little girl is tugging at my suit, her hand slips into mine and she pulls me over to sit with her. She has to be one of Mason and Katelyn's twins. The other one gets up and sits on my other side, holding my hand too. Katelyn looks at me and smiles. I don't know if she made this happen, but I'll be forever grateful.

This is my first funeral and hopefully my last. I never want to experience this ever again. As the pastor talks about Mason's life, I realize how much I've missed. When I look over at Noah, he's watching me and I wonder if he knows who I am. Did Josie ever tell him about me? Nick looks pissed and that sort of makes me laugh. I didn't like him in high school and the fact that he's holding my girl's hand isn't sitting all that well with me, but that's my issue and something I'll have to deal with.

I find it ironic that that he moved in on my girl when I wasn't around. If it was anyone else, I wouldn't care, but Ashford – it pisses me off.

"Is there anyone who would like to say a few things about Mason?"

I let go of the girls' hands and stand up, straightening out my jacket. People are whispering as I make my way to the podium, but I don't care. If I'm going to do this, I'm going to do it right.

I wink at Josie before clearing my throat and speaking into the microphone.

"Ten years ago I made the decision to change my life. In the process I lost the only family I truly cared about: Mason, Katelyn and Josie. I was selfish, confused and wanted away from the stigma of being Beaumont's golden boy. What I never banked on was losing Mason, my best friend since kindergarten. He was my partner in crime and my go-to on the field. Everything about my life and who I was growing up was because of Mason. When I heard that the world had lost him, a piece of me died. For the first time in a long time, I cried. I wept for every moment that I missed with him. I missed his engagement to Katelyn, his wedding and the birth of his beautiful girls who have opened their amazing hearts to me even though I don't deserve it. I let him down and for that I'll always be sorry.

"Mason, my friend, I'll do what I can to watch over your family and make sure they never want for anything."

Katelyn wraps her arms around me as soon as I make it back to the pew. The twins both grab a hold of my hand and squeeze tight.

"My name's Peyton. Will you watch football with me on Sunday?"

I look down at the little girl that is clearly all Mason with her Beaumont High football jersey on. "Hi Peyton, I'm Liam and I'd love to watch football with you."

JOSIE

Nick pulls me out of the church and into the parking lot. I knew he was pissed when I saw his face coming down the aisle, but it's not like I knew Liam was going to show up here. Nick walks us behind the church and swings me around so that my back is against the wall.

"How long, Josephine?" God I hate it when people use my full name. It's like I'm in trouble even though I'm an adult.

"He showed up last night."

"You didn't want to tell me?" I really thought Nick and I were better than this, that we had a stronger relationship.

"Nick, I'm not keeping anything from you. He showed up last night, we argued and he left. I didn't know he was going to be here today and honestly I'm more focused on Katelyn. Today isn't about Liam; it's about Katelyn and the girls."

"How does he know Noah?"

I take a deep breath. "I don't know," I answer truthfully.

I have my suspicions but I wasn't going to ask Liam and I'm definitely not bringing this up with Noah.

Nick starts pacing, pulling at his blond hair. He talks to himself. It looks like he's having a fight with an imaginary person.

"Tell Liam we want to meet with him later."

"Why?" I ask curiously. Nick stops in front of me and grabs my arms, pinning me to the wall. I've never seen him like this before. This is a side of him that I don't like.

"Because I'll have my lawyer draw up adoption papers and he can sign his parental rights away."

I can't believe my ears. I know he wants to adopt Noah, but we've never discussed it. I don't even know if this is something I want him to do. Noah's mine, he doesn't need to have Nick's last name. Even if we are married, things can stay the same between them.

"Um..."

"Hey guys, Noah's looking for you." I look over to find Jenna standing just a few feet away. Nick moves away, letting go of my arms. I try not to wince when the blood starts flowing again. I smile at Jenna to let her know that everything is fine.

"Thanks, Jenna." She smiles and walks away, leaving us to figure this shit out.

"Nick, just because Liam is here doesn't mean anything." I pull him into my arms. He relents and kisses me softly on the lips.

"I'm sorry, babe. I don't know what came over me. Seeing him here and winking at Noah, I just... my blood started to boil. He may have created that boy, but this is my family. The sooner he's gone the better."

"I agree, but let's not give him a reason to stay, okay?" Nick nods and leads me back to the crowd of people gathering. We find Noah and head to our car so we can follow the hearse and family car. The pall bearers need to be in line so they can be there too, standing guard, as my dad would say.

The funeral procession drives through the town, by the high school that has turned into a shrine for Mason. This week's game was postponed. It's the first time in Beaumont High history that the team won't be taking the field. Mason touched so many people this loss will be felt for years to come.

When we pull into the cemetery, some people have already gathered. I try not to look around for Liam when I get out of the car, but my eyes wander. He's spotted easily. He's the guy with the single and some not-so-single women standing around.

"Give me a break," Nick mutters as we get out of the car.

"It's not like he can turn off who he is, Nick. You don't see him signing autographs or anything. He's standing with the other guys."

"Are you defending him?"

I shake my head and grab Noah's hand. We walk over to Mason's burial site and find a spot to stand.

"Your flowers look great, Josie." A neighbor of Katelyn's comes up to me. I don't remember her name, but I should. I should know everyone in town. I thank her and she promises to stop by the shop.

"Mom, why are all those women talking to your old boyfriend?" I look at Noah and wonder how much he's figured out. I want to ask him where he met Liam, but that will have to wait. I can't help but look over at Liam. He looks at me and our eyes meet. I give him a soft smile and he shrugs.

"He's a musician. I guess they want his autograph."

"Well that's dumb. If I was famous and my friend died I wouldn't want to give out autographs."

"I bet Liam is thinking the same thing, baby."

AS WE DRIVE to Katelyn's to have Mason's celebration of life I'm baffled that she wanted to have it at their home. Nick and I offered ours, but she was adamant, saying Mason would've wanted a party at his house.

A party?

I don't feel like having a party. I feel like curling up in my oversized chair, wrapping myself in a blanket and watching old home movies. Nick has caught me doing that a few times since Mason left us, each time the look on his face the same. I knew he wasn't happy I was watching. That he was probably questioning my devotion to him; those weren't our memories but mine and Liam's.

We are well into the "party" as Mason would've called it when Liam walks in. I'm trying not to judge, but he has a harem of girls following him. I can't tell if he likes this or not. I used to know what every one of his facial features meant, but it's been so long.

Peyton runs up to Liam and pulls on his suit jacket. He smiles and bends down so that he's level with her. He pulls on one of her pigtails and she lets out the most amazing laugh.

"Are thems your girlfriends?"

I can't help but laugh and lean closer so I can hear the answer. Half of me would like to know more about him, but the other half, the logical half, doesn't want to care and can't wait for him to leave.

Liam looks at those women and grimaces. "No, I don't know them. Are they friends of yours?"

Peyton shakes her head. Liam leans in and whispers something to her causing her to laugh again.

"'Cuse me, do you know my daddy?"

One of the women throws her head back and laughs as if this particular question is the funniest she's ever heard. "No, we don't, but we'd like to." She turns and looks at her friends and they all giggle. Don't they realize where they are?

Peyton steps forward, her hands on her hips. Before she has a chance to say anything, Katelyn appears out of nowhere. "I'm sorry I don't think we've met. How did you know Mason?"

"Oh, we don't. We heard that Liam Page was going to be at this party and as luck would have it he was just getting out of his car when we pulled up."

The look on Liam's face is so uncomfortable that I feel sorry for him. He's holding Peyton's hand, not even looking at the women behind him.

"Unfortunately this isn't your lucky day. Liam Page isn't here and doesn't live in Beaumont so you might want try catching him on tour or something."

The three of them start laughing, one of them pointing. "That right there is Liam Page. I swear my life on it."

Katelyn looks at Liam who is full of remorse. I'm simply amazed at her ability to stay calm and cool. Nick kisses me on my cheek and steps toward Liam.

"Westbury, want to toss the ball around?"

Liam looks at Nick and nods. When he spots me standing along the wall watching this entire exchange his expression is unreadable.

"Well, would you look at that, his name is Westbury.

Out you go." I step forward and help Katelyn usher the women out of the house.

"I'm so sorry, Katelyn." I've never had to apologize for Liam before. I'm not sure why I'm doing it now.

Katelyn waves her hand as if it's no big deal. "It was only a matter of time before someone blabbed that he was in town. Things may be strained, but not today. Mason would've wanted him here."

I don't know if she's taking a jab at me or not. Maybe I should've called everyone last night and told them that he was back, but I didn't know if he'd be here today. Hell, I didn't even know if he knew about Mason. I suppose I could've told them, but I was more worried about saving my son from the impending heartache.

A ball flying past the window catches my attention. I walk outside and my heart stops because in one space is the man I once loved, the man I'm going to marry and the one that ties us all together and they're playing football.

I t seems of late I'm making mistakes with every turn. Stopping at the store was today's mistake. I should've known better. I should've gone straight to Katelyn's, but I didn't want to show up empty handed.

And now I'm in this awkward situation in the backyard with Nick Ashford and my son. A son that doesn't know I'm his dad. Hell, Josie won't even confirm he's mine but I can see it when I look at him, he's the best of me and Josie regardless of how he ended up here or how our lives have taken different paths.

And who knew Nick would come to my rescue? He has to know I want to kick his ass for touching my girl, but by the way she looks at him she must be okay with it.

"What happened in there?"

I said I would come out and play ball, but never agreed to chat. I could ignore him, pretend we're back in high school and this new kid is trying to fit in with the rest of us. We had our group and we were tight.

But I don't do that. Not today.

"I figured I'd be able to run into the store, grab something from the bakery, pick up some flowers and get Katelyn her favorite wine from when we were in school.

"As soon as I got to the check-out I began to realize my mistake. No disguise. No fake eyeglasses or hat to pull down over my eyes. The young cashier took one look at me and she knew. Before it was even my turn, she had already texted someone and I knew I was doomed."

"'*Sorry about your friend*' was all she said while she scanned my items a bit too slowly. When I pulled up in front there were these girls right behind me, following me in." I throw the ball back to Nick who just shakes his head. "This is the last thing I wanted for Katelyn, especially today."

"Does it happen a lot?"

I take off my jacket and unbutton my shirt so I don't ruin it. Noah's eyes stare at the tattoos on my arms and I wonder if I'll ever be able to sit down with him and have a conversation. Tell him about me and maybe have a relationship with him.

"I don't go out much when I'm home. It will happen on tour, but I'm not in one place long enough for it to really matter."

I can feel people staring at me; it's something I'm used to, but here it seems odd. When I look over at the patio Josie is standing there. All five foot nine of her, add a few inches with her heels. She's kept herself looking good after high school, her legs look toned and her stomach still as flat as I remember. Nick clears his throat in the background and I can't help but laugh. I'd be doing the same thing if someone was ogling my girlfriend, but he forgets that I had her first.

"Wanna go put on a little skirt and cheer for us, Josie?" her face falls and I know she didn't enjoy my little joke. I try to laugh it off, but she's not buying it. She looks at Nick who is furious with me and shakes her head. I watch as she walks back into the house, her ass looking as tight as ever. I shake my head to clear the memories that were about to start creeping in.

"Mr. Westbury, do you still play football?" I peel my eyes off the retreating backside of my ex to look at my son. I want to reach out and touch him, run my hands through his hair and ask him every conceivable question known to man, but I don't. I need to talk to Josie so we can figure this shit out. If she thinks I'm going to forget that he exists, she has another thing coming.

"Nah, I don't have much time. What about you, do you play?"

He nods furiously and points to Nick. "My dad, Nick, coaches my team." I've been pretty relaxed with him dating Josie because I gave her up. I don't have much say, but my son calling him dad? I can't have that. I wasn't told that I had a son. If I had I would've been here.

"Is that so?" I ask pushing down the anger that is boiling. I know I can't fault the kid for calling Nick 'dad,' it's my fault, but Josie shouldn't allow it. She knows that I would've been here if I knew about him. We talked about kids all the time, we both wanted them, so it's not like I would've bailed on her.

Even if I did the unthinkable and left her, it's not like I didn't love her. Leaving her broke my heart too.

Noah nods and seems very excited to tell me about Nick even if I don't want to hear it. "I play quarterback. That was your position and your record still stands from when you were in high school. No one is even close to breaking it, at least that's what uncle Mason said."

I crouch down and look at Noah and smile. I smile at the thought of Noah calling Mason his uncle. The football player in me is excited that he loves the game. I loved the game at his age and wanted to play all the time. The adult in me hopes that Josie has him in other activities because there is so much more to life than football.

"Do you have a three or a five step drop?" I ask, curious just how much Nick has taught him.

"I have both, would you like to see?" he asks eagerly. I hold out the football for him to take, watching as he grips the laces like he was born to be a quarterback.

"Here it comes, Nick," he yells and I'm taken back by the fact that he didn't call him dad. I watch both routines and notice that he's a natural, much better than I was at his age. I can only hope Josie lets him make the best decision for his life unlike my father. I'd hate for him to resent her and not have a relationship with his parents over a life altering decision.

When I think of my parents I wonder if they know Noah. Are they a part of his life? Have they been watching my boy grow up without me?

"Wow, you're so much better than I was at your age."

Noah smiles and when he does he looks just like Josie. "Thanks. My mom says I'm a natural and that it's in my blood."

"Yeah, I think your mom is right."

Nick walks off, leaving Noah and I to talk. I ask him if he wants to sit down and maybe eat some lunch and he agrees. We stand next to each other and I watch what he puts on his plate. He piles it high with veggies, crackers, cheese and some pasta dish. I add everything that he does because those are all my favorite foods too.

There are chairs set up outside and, even though it's a crisp day, the sun is providing just enough heat that we can sit out here and relax.

"So, what's it like to be famous, Mr. Westbury." I stiffen at 'mister'. In fact, I hate it. And I hate that he asked about being famous because I never wanted to be famous. I just wanted to make music. I wanted to try my hand at something different just to see if I could succeed.

"You can call me Liam," I reply. "And being famous is okay. I work hard and sometimes I'm away from where I live for a long time."

"My friend Johnny says rock stars have like twenty girlfriends and you came with three girls. Are they yours?" If I didn't know better I'd think his mother put him up to this.

"No, I don't have a girlfriend or a wife. I have a cat, but he doesn't like me too much."

Noah starts laughing, his legs swinging on the chair. I want to reach out and put my hand on his knees just like I used to do Josie. Although she's so tall she could only do this from the tailgate on my truck.

"Your cat doesn't like you? How come?"

I shrug. "I don't know. He's very mean though and I think about telling him to pack his kitty bags and move out."

"Where is he now?"

"He's in Los Angeles where I live. I have a housekeeper that will feed him while I'm gone."

"Where does he sleep?"

Odd question coming from a boy. "He has one of those cat palace things. Maybe that's why he hates me – because it's a palace and not a race car or something like that."

Listening to Noah laugh has quickly become like music to my ears. I want to record it and listen to it over and over while I write. Looking at him inspires me to write about him, capture him in song.

"So, what about you? Do you have a girlfriend, wife or a cat that hates you?"

"No, I don't have any of those. My mom says that maybe after her and Nick get married we can get a dog."

Married? I bite back a string of slurs that want to fly out of my mouth when he talks about Nick and Josie. I know I can't say anything. I gave her up, but I won't lie and say it doesn't hurt to see her with someone else. I don't know what I expected, maybe for her to be miserable and as lost as I am.

JOSIE

I never thought I'd see this day. I've had many dreams of the day Noah would meet Liam, but never like this. I resigned myself to thinking Noah would look up Liam when he turned eighteen. They could fight or bond or do whatever it is fathers and sons do when they first meet each other. The only thing I didn't want was for Noah to hate Liam for not being around. I could've tried harder to tell him, but I didn't. I was selfish and wanted to hear his voice. I wanted him to hear my voice and come home. I was angry and it took me a long time to get over that anger.

Now watching them outside, deep in conversation I want to wrap them up in a tight bubble so they can never be away from each other. I know that's not fair to Liam – he has a life away from here that's vastly different. He's different, yet so much the same boy that I fell in love with all those years ago.

The boy I never stopped loving.

Looking at Noah and Liam side by side, there's no denying they're son and father.

Liam keeps eye contact with Noah each time they talk.

I know Nick is pissed that Liam is here and honestly so am I, but what can I do? Noah knows who Liam is from living in Beaumont. He just doesn't know who he is and I think I want to leave it that way, at least for now. Liam will be gone soon and we'll all go back to normal.

"What are you thinking?" Katelyn rests her head inside the crook of my elbow. Her small, five-foot-two frame that doesn't quite reach my shoulder allows me to wrap my arm around her, pulling her closer.

"I'm not sure," I say. "There are too many emotions flowing through me."

"He looks just like him," she says keeping her voice low and away from prying guests. "What are you going to do?"

I shake my head because I don't know. I haven't a clue what I should do. My brain is saying ignore it and Liam will go away again, but my heart is telling me to go out there and demand that he be part of Noah's life. It's the least he can do since he's been absent for the past ten years.

"He'll be gone soon. Maybe I'll just let him call the shots."

"Not too soon, sweetie. He's watching football with Peyton on Sunday. A lot can happen in three days." Katelyn kisses me on the cheek and leaves me to stare out the window at two of the three boys that own my heart.

THE DRIVE HOME from Katelyn's was quiet. Nick held my hand and Noah fell asleep before we pulled away from the house. He spent the rest of the day talking to Liam about stats and perfect field position while Nick watched from the sidelines. I know there were a few snide remarks made to Nick, but he brushed them off.

"What are you thinking about?" Nick asks as he slides into bed. He props himself up on his elbow, clearly ready to discuss everything that has happened today. I just want to go to bed.

"You know Katelyn asked me the same thing earlier. She was more concerned about me when I should've been taking care of her."

"She knows you love her." He places his hand on my waist, bunching my silk pajamas into his fist. "Today was..."

"Difficult, sad, not expected, odd. I could go on and on, but nothing really sums up what today was. A clusterfuck, maybe?" I shift closer to Nick and he brings his arm around me, pulling me closer. His lips trail down my neck until he reaches my lips, kissing me softly.

"We should talk about Liam and Noah. I know I'm not Noah's dad, but I want to be, you know this. I was wrong for the way I acted today, so very wrong for lashing out at you about Liam and I'm sorry."

"I know you are." I run my fingers through his hair. "I don't think Liam will want to be a part of Noah's life right now, but maybe later. Maybe we should just leave it alone; he'll be gone soon."

Nick pushes my hair behind my ear. He cups my chin and pulls me closer. "I love you, Josie," he says before kissing me. His kiss is soft, not rushed, like he's taking his time to memorize me. Almost as if he's desperate.

I love him, I do. But seeing Liam with Noah I can't help but wonder about what the future holds and how Nick and I can fit together.

"Hey Josie!" Katelyn and I turn around to see Liam Westbury walking toward us. Katelyn is a traitor and leaves my side. She's laughing as she walks away. My palms are sweating and my legs suddenly feel like jello.

This year I finally noticed him. He grew up so much over the summer that I really didn't pay attention before when we were at Katelyn's house. Then he went away to football camp for a month and came back totally hot.

I've been dying for him to take off his shirt just once so I can have a clear visual of his abs because my imagination just isn't cutting it.

"Hey," he says. He's holding his football helmet in one hand. The other is tugging at the collar of his jersey, one that I want to rip off.

"Hey," I say stupidly.

"How was the rest of your summer?"

"It was good. I read a lot." I read a lot? Oh my god he's going to think I'm a nerd. What the hell is wrong with me? The ground has suddenly become very interesting as I stare at my shoe while it pushes a rock around.

My skin tingles when he lifts my chin, his sky blue eyes boring into mine and all I can think about is jumping into his arms and stuffing my tongue into his mouth. I'm only fifteen, but I've watched movies. I'm sure I can figure it out.

"Will you go to homecoming with me?"

"Homecoming?" My mind can barely comprehend what he's asking. But I swear to god he said homecoming. As in get all dressed up and dance. That means he wants to dance with me, hold me against his body and sway to cheesy love songs. The same love songs I play at night when I'm writing Josephine Westbury in my notebook.

"Yeah. I have my driver's license now so I can drive and I thought—"

"Yes!" He jumps and starts laughing. "Sorry," I say covering my face with my hands.

He pulls my hands away but doesn't let go of them.

When he leans forward I feel as if I'm going to pass out. He smells like Old Spice, my new favorite smell.

"Please don't cover your face. You're far too gorgeous to hide." He kisses me on the cheek before walking toward the field. "I'll call you tonight." He turns back and yells before he takes off running.

I wake up in a cold sweat with tears streaming down my face. Nick is snoring softly beside me, his arm pinning me to the bed. I maneuver out from underneath him and make my way to the bathroom.

With the light off, I sit on the edge of the tub and cry into a towel, muffling my sobs. I never thought I'd see the boy who stole my heart and failed to give it back.

I'm not sure I want it back.

When I leave Katelyn's house I decide to stop at the store. This time I don't care who sees me because if some tart in a tight little dress wants to follow me she can. Hell she can bring her friends as long as they bring alcohol. I grab a case of beer, chips and some candy and set it gently on the conveyor belt. There is an older woman working now so I think I'm in the clear. I highly doubt she listens to my music or even knows who I am for that matter.

I hold my breath, hoping she doesn't ask for my driver's license. I make very little eye contact with her and offer her a few strategically timed smiles as she swipes my items.

"Does your mama know you're back in town?"

I study the cashier to see if I can place her. Her name tag says 'Shirley' and I rack my brain. I can't remember her, but that doesn't mean I can't play along.

"No, ma'am," I reply, trying to be as polite as possible. She eyes the tattoos on my arms, probably looking for the one that says MOM. Sadly, she won't find one on my body.

"No, I don't suppose she does. Seems since word broke

out that you're in town, the girls around here are in a bit of a frenzy."

"I don't mean to rile anyone up. Just came to pay my respects."

"Such a shame what happened to Mason. Sure hope Katelyn can take care of those babies."

I nod and start wishing that she'll hurry up. I don't really want to chat. I want to drink away my sorrows and pay tribute to my friend.

"Katelyn will be just fine." I'll make sure of it.

"Yeah, I suppose with all your fancy music money you can step up and take care of her."

I take a deep breath and roll my neck. I won't lose my patience. When she finally tells me my total, I hand her a twenty and tell her to keep the change. Now she has a nice little tip from my fancy music money.

"Tell my mom I say hi when you see her." I pick up my items and walk away and her mouth hangs open. Stupid town gossip. After today everyone will know I'm here and I can't leave for another few days. I made a promise to Peyton and I intend to keep it.

The drive is familiar and when I pull into the field I let out a sigh of relief that no one is here. I climb the ladder, my beer and snacks in the plastic bag. I get to the top and hold onto the railing, looking out over the field. I never appreciated the view when I was spending every Friday night here. The view in the parking lot is what kept my attention. Josie and her long legs, always bare because we'd come right from the game. I'd change, but she always kept her cheerleading outfit on. She knew how much I liked it.

I sit in my same spot. My finger traces the heart with mine and Josie's initials in it. I put that there after homecoming our sophomore year. I knew that night I wanted this girl in my life forever and wasn't afraid to tell her.

Until I left her when I should've packed her bags for her and carried her to my truck.

I wonder if Josie would've liked Los Angeles.

I down my first, then second beer. If I had my truck I'd be shooting the empties into the back just so I could hear them shatter. So I can have some type of relief from this building pain.

When a truck pulls in and backs up, I know my time is over. I close my eyes and wait for the laughter to appear. Mason and I were so loud the girls were always telling us to shut up. I don't see who got out of the truck, but can hear them climbing the ladder.

Lovely.

"What are you doing here?" I look over and see Katelyn walking toward me. I stand and offer her my hand until she sits down in what would've been Mason's spot, on my left.

"I should be asking you the same thing. Why aren't you home with those beautiful babies?"

"They are with Mason's dad tonight. He wanted to have them and I can't say no. He's lost so much in the past year."

I look at her questioningly. She smiles sadly. "Mrs. Powell died last year."

And the knife just keeps twisting.

"I'm sorry," I say simply because I have nothing else to say. There is no excuse for what I've done.

"Where ya been, Liam?"

Well now that's the million dollar question because if you watch TV or read the magazines while waiting to check out at the local mart, everyone knows where I've been.

"You gotta be a little more specific than that," I reply as I throw my first empty into the bed of the truck.

Katelyn reaches into my bag, grabs a beer and pops the top.

"What happened to you? Because when you went off to Texas everything was fine and then you show up one night and everything isn't?"

I throw my second empty into the truck. My third follows and I open my fourth and chug it down to throw it.

"I got to school and hated it. I hated practice, the team, everything about it. And one night I went to this on campus hang-out and there was an open mic night so I gave it a try and I liked it and I don't know."

"Did you tell Josie?"

"Nah, our meeting didn't go so well the other night. I was pissed and antagonized her a bit."

We sit in silence, drinking and throwing our bottles into the truck. Katelyn's throws get harder and harder the more she drinks and I imagine she's taking out some type of anger.

"For the first time in twelve years I don't have Mason by my side."

I know she's sad and I could hold her and let her cry or I can share in her misery.

"I have a kid."

Apparently that was the wrong thing to say because if looks could kill I'd be dead right now.

"Does Josie know?"

I can't help but laugh. I shake my head. "I hope so, unless Noah isn't hers. Then I'm screwed because that boy is definitely mine and definitely hers."

"You're such an ass," she says pushing my shoulder. I fall back so she thinks she's strong. "No other kids, huh? How many wives and girlfriends do you have?"

I toss my empty down to the truck and smile when it

shatters. I'm going to have to go over and clean out her truck tomorrow.

"No other kids, no wives and no girlfriends."

"Right now?"

I look at her and give her the stink eye. "Ever. Never. Not since Josie."

"I've seen those rags with your picture on them and you have some blond with you all the time."

I lean against the tower and sip on my next beer. Katelyn is keeping up with me and we'll be out soon. This sort of pisses me off. I should've bought two cases.

"That's Sam, my manager. She wants to be my girl-friend and tells me that I owe her since she's been with me since I started. I don't know. Lately I've been thinking about firing her."

Katelyn doesn't say anything; she just stares out into the darkness. Every now and again I see her wipe her eyes. I want to help her but don't know how. I could wrap my arms around her, pull her into a hug, but that might be awkward for her so I opt to rub her back.

"I'll never forgive myself. I should've called or at least come back. I could've kept in touch but leaving here and leaving everything behind – I needed a clean break. I had to try and make a name for myself and when I did, people just kept pushing and pulling and the next thing I know I'm in my hotel room and I'm reading the paper. I kept saying to myself there is no fucking way he's gone because I didn't get to say good-bye.

"He's gone and I never got a chance to tell him how fucking sorry I am for being a total dick and leaving. Mason didn't do jack shit to me and I left him because I'm a fucking coward and couldn't face the bullshit going on in my life. God, I'm so sorry you lost him."

Katelyn leans back and buries her face in my chest. She starts to sob so I put my arms around her and let her cry. I wipe away the tears that have let loose and try to be strong for her. The more she cries, the more I do. Maybe crying is therapeutic, maybe your body needs it to expel the pent up energy. Maybe we just need to cry for Mason.

We stay like this, holding each other, until the sun starts to come up. Her face is red and streaked from smeared make-up. Lines are creased on her face from my jacket, but I don't care. I continue to hold her until she's ready to say good-bye.

For the first time, I'm closing the shop for no reason. My lack of sleep is evident by the dark bags under my eyes. Nick felt my forehead, always in doctor mode, before leaving for work and suggested I take a day for myself. I opted to give Jenna another day off as well. No one needs flowers today anyway and if they do, they'll understand why I'm closed and come back tomorrow.

Noah is crunching away on his cereal, his eyes glued to his recent *Sports Illustrated*. Yesterday I watched him and Liam with reservation, but still allowed them to get to know each other. Today I've decided that was enough. I can't have my son getting hurt when Liam skips town again. He isn't planning on staying, whether he's told me this or not. I just know it. I feel it in my heart. He has a life away from Beaumont, one that doesn't include Noah and likely never will.

I pour myself a cup of coffee and sit down across from Noah. He doesn't look up, completely enthralled in whatever article he's reading. Guaranteed it's about football. I tried to discourage him, suggest he play soccer but he wouldn't hear of it. He's been a natural and it scares me. I see so much of Liam in him and I don't want to.

"Did you know Liam Westbury was on the cover of Sports Illustrated when he was in high school?"

I spit out my coffee, the hot liquid dribbling down my chin. How does he know this? Nick and I, as well as Mason and Katelyn, have never discussed Liam with Noah. I can't even remember a time when Liam's name has come up. We've always skirted around that name. I secretly chide the teachers at school always praising Liam for everything he's done for Beaumont and football.

"Guess what?"

Liam wraps his arms around me from behind, nuzzling my neck. "What?" I ask as I set my books on the shelf in my locker. I catch a glimpse of our junior prom picture – Liam in his black tux and me in my red knee-length dress.

"Someone is going to be on the cover of Sports Illustrated."

I turn and wrap my arms around him. I know he's wanted this since last year when he came close to breaking the state record for passing yards and he's close again this year. "I'm so proud of you."

"I couldn't have done it without my girl," he says before kissing me full on the lips, a big no-no in the hallway.

"We should go celebrate."

"What are you thinking?" he asks suggestively.

I shrug, pushing my fingers into his recently shaved head. His eyes close as I massage his scalp. He loves it when I do this.

"Are your parent's home?" he asks and when I shake my head no. He pulls one of my hands into his and walks us out of the school.

"How do you know?" I ask barely able to get the words out without choking.

"I saw the cover at the museum on our field trip."

"Is that where you met Liam the other day?" My curiosity piques. When Liam showed up at the shop I had no idea how he found out about Noah.

Noah nods. "I was upset over a thing they had for Mason and he was in the bathroom. We talked and I said he was the guy kissing you in the video. Was he your boyfriend?"

Do I answer or deflect? Or do I just come out and say he's your dad and totally ditched us when I was pregnant even though I never told him. Yeah that won't work.

"I don't want you talking to Liam Westbury anymore."

"Why not?" Noah deadpans.

"Because... because I said so that's why." I get up and move back into the kitchen and dump out my coffee. It no longer tastes very good and isn't doing its job. I just want to crawl into bed and forget this conversation ever started.

Noah slams his magazine down on the table, spilling the rest of his cereal. He sits there, stewing, not moving an inch to clean up his mess.

"Are you going to clean that?" I ask before throwing him a dishtowel. Anger flashes in his eyes. I know I've upset him, but he's just too young to understand the magnitude of this situation. Liam is going to hurt him,

"No," he says without making eye contact.

"Excuse me?"

He pushes his chair out and picks up his magazine. He turns and looks at me, a look I've never seen from my precious boy. His face is red, his breathing is labored.

"I like Liam," he yells.

I'm taken aback by his outburst. If this is how he's going

to be after two encounters there is no way I can let Liam into his life.

"Liam doesn't live here, Noah, and once he's gone you won't see him again. Let it go."

"Why do you hate him?"

I don't, that's the problem and I wish I did, but he's a disruption and he's already ruining things in my house and I don't want that. I can't have that.

"I don't hate him," I mumble. I press my fingertips to my temple to hopefully ward off the impending headache.

"You used to kiss him, a lot. I've seen the DVD's. How can you kiss someone so much and not like him?" Noah stands in front of me, his arms clutching his magazine. His eyes are trained on me and all I see is Liam.

"That was a long time ago, Noah. People change. I've changed and so has Liam. We aren't friends anymore and I don't want you talking to him. I'm the adult here and I make the rules. Liam Westbury is off limits."

"You're not being fair. I like him and he's good at football just like me. He can help me get better and he said he would come to my game today!" My heart breaks at the sight of his tears, but I'd take this one day of tears over the months of tears he'll cry when Liam leaves him. I reach out for Noah, but he moves away and runs off to his room. I'm going to have to find a way to get a hold of Liam and tell him he can't come to the game. That he needs to just ignore Noah for all of our sakes. It will be easier that way.

At least that is what I tell myself.

When the doorbell rings I rush to let in Katelyn. She takes one look at me and shakes her head, pulling me into her arms.

"What am I going to do?" I ask Katelyn. I lead her into the kitchen, sitting down. She's across from me, holding my hand when I should be holding hers. I should be her rock right now. She's just lost her husband and here I am complaining to her.

"I'm not sure I can answer that for you," she says, her eyes full of pity. I really need to stop thinking about myself and start thinking about her.

"I'm sorry. I shouldn't be dumping this on you. You have enough to deal with." I remove my hand and start cleaning up our mess. I invited her over for breakfast, not problem solving.

"I'm your friend, Josie. You can dump anything on me."

I shake my head and leave her sitting at the table. She comes and stands next to me while the sink fills with hot sudsy water.

"I remember everything so clearly. It's like all my memories are this vivid coloring book turned into a nightmare. I dreamt about him last night and I haven't done that since Noah was about two. I stopped reading the magazines and looking for the music videos because I needed a clean break and now he's here for the next few days and there's nothing I can do to keep him from coming to Noah's game tonight."

"Have you thought about sitting down with him and talking to him about Noah?" she asks as I start washing the dishes. I soak my hands in the water and relish the feel of the burn from the hot water.

"I don't think I can." I sigh and lean my head against hers. "Nick wants Liam to sign some adoption papers or something like that, but I don't know. Nick and I haven't discussed this and I fear it's a knee-jerk reaction to Liam showing up in town."

Katelyn takes my hands in hers and pulls them out of the water. We're dripping water and soap bubbles travel down the front of our clothes and onto the floor. She holds them tight, her eyes brimming with tears.

"I lost my husband last week and wasn't able to say good-bye. You are being given a second chance and whether you make that chance just about Noah or to find some closure for yourself you owe it to the three of you to find a happy medium. If Noah was to ever find out that Liam is his dad and you didn't tell him while he has this one chance to know him, he'll never forgive you, Josie, and you'll never forgive yourself."

"Liam is going to hurt him," I say through tears.

"Liam might surprise you if you give him a chance."

We end up spending the rest of the afternoon at her house avoiding the topic of Liam. Katelyn decided she wanted to tackle the man room in the basement and we're marking things that she thinks Mason's friends will like. When I come to Liam's name on the list I have to fight the tears – it's like she's forgiven him for everything without a second thought – because Liam is getting Mason's Most Valuable Player trophy that he earned in college.

He gave me the time and place and asked me to come watch him. Said I could give him some pointers on his five-step drop at halftime. I want to do this, I do, but I don't know. Josie made it crystal clear she wants me to have nothing to do with him and I don't see her knocking on my door asking me to claim him.

But I want to watch him play. I want to remember what it was like to love the game and maybe I'll learn to love it again now that I have a reason to watch – if I'm even allowed to have this reason. Josie holds all the cards where Noah is concerned.

The last time I sat down for a game was Mason's last one as a senior. I never had a chance to tell him, but I never missed a game, watching him on television every Saturday. A few times I thought about showing up to one, but I wasn't ready to face anyone. Apparently, I'm still not since I can't have a decent conversation or be in the same room with Josie without pissing her off.

But she's so feisty when she's upset. I miss that. I miss seeing the fire in her eyes when she's determined to prove me wrong. I miss the passion in her body when she's trying to show me what it's like to be loved by her. I'd give anything to feel that with her again, even if it's just for one fleeting, solitary moment. Just one quick taste of my girl again and I'd be complete.

I'm a liar.

I've been lying to myself since the day I left Beaumont. I walked away from the one great thing in my life because I was selfish enough to think I didn't need her and that she'd be better off without me.

And if I could, I'd go back and change it all.

"Hello?"

"Liam?" I look at my phone, confused by the number showing on the display.

"Yeah, who's this?"

"This is Betty Addison, your grandmother."

I pull the phone away again and look at the screen. Maybe I didn't hear her properly, but I swear she said grandmother. I only know my father's side of the family. My mother never talked about her parents.

"Um... okay," I say not sure what else to add.

"I'm in town this week and I thought we could have lunch. There's a nice little café by your campus."

What do I have to lose and it's free lunch. "Sure," I say. We set the date and time to meet. We talk a bit more and she asked that I hear her out before making any judgment calls as to why she's been absent for the last eighteen years of my life.

I agree.

I'm nervous as I wait for her, my leg bounces. The same annoying habit I've picked up from Josie. When the chair in front of me pulls out and she sits down I see an older version of my mother. Or what I envision my mom will look like.

"It's so nice to finally meet you," she says while studying my face.

Conversation is awkward at first as we get to know each other but half an hour in it's like I've known her my entire life. We sit and talk for hours. My grandma tells me she's an actress, but hasn't acted in years. When I ask about my mom and why they don't talk, she shows me a picture of Bianca. She's dressed as a starlet, holding a trophy. Betty says it's her Rising Star Award, she won it at sixteen.

"She never told me."

"When she met your father she gave up her dreams for his. I fought hard to make her see what she was doing, but your father was determined to have a trophy wife on his arm and your mother would do anything to please him."

I sit and listen to my grandma tell me about a mom that I don't even know. The last thing Betty says to me that day is something I will never forget. "Follow only your dreams, Liam."

One phone call and a few hours changed my life and it's questionable whether that change was for the best.

I could be living happily with Noah now, raising him and coaching his football team. Josie would be my wife. I was going to marry that girl and she knew it. Hell, our parents knew it and mine hated it. They didn't like that Josie's parents didn't have the social status they did and didn't belong to the stuffy country club, but I didn't care. That girl rocked my world.

And I'm willing to bet she still does.

I decide to clean Katelyn's truck. I don't want her messing with the broken beer bottles and I certainly don't want the twins climbing in the back and cutting themselves. This is the least I can do for her after she's opened her heart and home to me.

Last night, holding her, for the first time I felt like I could belong somewhere. I could be me without having to put on a show. Like Liam Westbury could exist again, but maybe this time I could combine him with Liam Page.

Just as I finish sweeping up the glass and disposing of it, the alarm on my phone goes off. I know it's telling me that Noah's game is about to start and I need to make a decision. Do I go and risk Josie getting pissed? Or do I go and show my boy that while I may not be around, I do intend to keep my word?

I make the only decision possible.

My bike rumbles as I hit the starter wishing I had kept the rental or at least had my truck. I wonder if my parents kept my truck. I could go ask, but that means visiting and I'm not so sure I'm ready to face them yet. I wasn't in Los Angeles three days before my dad had my truck taken away. I'm sure Sterling and Bianca Westbury won't be so glad to see their straight-laced son show up on a motorcycle with his tattoos showing. But then again maybe a trip to the country club is in order.

The drive through town is becoming familiar. I used to dream of these streets at night until my dreams just became hazy and convoluted. After a while you just forget. You forget that old lady Williams never takes down her Christmas decorations even though the town begs her to do it. You forget that the whole town shuts down for Friday night football. People don't forget you though and what you've done, both on the field and off.

When I pull up to the school, the bleachers are packed. The sound of my bike gets their attention, something I wanted to avoid. I take off my helmet and slide on my ball cap and fake eyeglasses. I'm sure the disguise isn't needed, but if I don't look like Liam Page maybe they'll leave me alone.

Katelyn waves to me from the stands, her face looks sad. Josie is sitting next to her, but she doesn't look and I'm okay with that. I haven't earned a wave or a smile from her... yet.

I avoid the bleachers, opting to stand against the old oak tree that has been on this field long before I was old enough to play here. I hear Nick on the side, calling out plays and can see Noah when he takes center. I stand a bit taller when I see his number. He's wearing the same number I wore: eight. I swallow hard and clear my throat. I don't want to show any emotion and I'm sure it's just coincidence. But what if it's not?

Peyton comes over halfway through the game and hangs with me. She holds a football under her arm and is wearing cleats. I remind myself to ask Katelyn if she plays football. I can totally see Mason allowing his daughter to play. I'd ask her, but I don't want to give her any ideas. I laugh when she calls out plays or yells at the refs to 'flow a flag'. As I watch her, I see so much of Mason in her and wonder how Katelyn is going to manage. I start to wonder about their financial situation and if there is any way I can help. I know Katelyn won't take a hand-out, but I'll figure something out. I don't want to see them struggle and I have the means to help them.

The final whistle blows and Noah is jumping up and down. I can't help but smile and feel a little bit proud even though I didn't do any of it. Watching him out there lead his team at this young age, he's showing so much promise. I can only hope he'll be better than I was and actually follow through with college and his promises.

I feel an ache in my heart when he comes running over

to me, his helmet in his hand and his hair matted down with sweat. He looks like I did after a game.

"You came?" he says it as if he didn't expect me to.

"I said I would. Sorry I was late I had some things to do first."

"No, that's okay. I'm just glad you got to see me play before you left town."

I was supposed to leave this morning, but promised Peyton football. Sunday is still a few days away and I haven't checked in with Sam. She's expecting me tomorrow.

"I'll be here until the end of the week. Miss Peyton and I have a date on Sunday in front of her TV."

"To watch football?"

I nod.

"Cool, maybe I can come too?"

I look at Peyton who eyes Noah. "That would be up to Peyton. Maybe you guys should talk about it."

Noah looks at Peyton and smiles. She rolls her eyes. I start laughing. I see romance in their future. Noah watches as Peyton runs over to Katelyn. "So how did I do?" he asks when he turns back to me.

"You did well. You released too early on a few plays, but that is just a matter of you and your receiver getting your timing down. You guys just need to practice your routes and you'll be fine."

"Wow. This is so cool getting tips from you."

"Noah what did I say?" Noah freezes when Josie speaks. I look at her; her face is stern and determined. She's not walking toward us, she's stomping.

"Liam was just giving me advice."

Josie barely makes eye contact with me and I realize this is going to get ugly. Her expression tells me everything I need to know; she's not going to let me see Noah.

"Go to the car, Noah. Now!" Josie points much like those mothers we used to make fun of when we were younger.

I don't move a muscle. I wait until Noah is far enough away before I move toward her.

"Don't come any closer, Liam. I mean it. I don't know what game you're playing, but it stops now and I want you gone. You need to leave and just forget about Noah."

"What the hell are you talking about? He asked me to come and I said I would. I would've been here the whole time if I knew, but I didn't. So don't come at me with this bullshit game, Josie. You kept him from me and, yeah I get that you couldn't get a hold of me on my cell, but there were other ways.

"Get off your high horse, Josephine, because if you fall it won't be pretty." I stuff my hands into my pocket and walk away. I didn't want to blow up at her, but she egged me on.

"I tried!" I stop and turn around.

"Is that so?"

"Yeah it is." She stands with hands on her hips and I know she's full of shit.

"I'm sure you did."

14

JOSIE

Watching his backside as he retreats should be second nature for me. This isn't the first time he's walked away from me and likely won't be the last. If I'm lucky he'll be gone for another ten years and I won't have to deal with him anymore.

He frustrates me to no end with his cocky ass I don't give a shit attitude. Doesn't he know he's messing with my kid? He knows he has no intentions on staying and playing make-up daddy, so why is he even trying now? Why can't he just go back to wherever it is that he came from and leave us the hell alone?

"You're going to break your fingernails if you clutch your hands any tighter." Katelyn smirks at me as she walks by. Peyton turns and gives me a dirty look. Lovely, so she heard me tell Liam to get out of town. I know she asked him to watch football with her, but seriously Katelyn should want her as far away from Liam as possible.

"Stop taking his side," I say as I stalk behind Katelyn. I'm a coward and say it to her back because I don't want to see her disappointed look. Noah is already in the backseat when I climb into my car. He stares at the window, avoiding eye contact. His arms are crossed over his chest as he sighs repeatedly. I'm not changing my mind. I don't care how long he ignores me for.

We have to sit and wait for Nick to get done talking with parents. I seethe when I see Candy Appleton touch Nick's arm. She's always wanted what's mine; first Liam and now Nick. I press the horn, alerting him that I'm waiting. I'm in no mood to sit in this parking lot while they make goo-goo eyes at each other.

"What's your problem?" Nick asks when he finally gets into the car. I should've walked home. I thought about it. I could've used the time to cool off and get my thoughts together.

"She's mad because I was talking to Liam," Noah blurts out causing Nick to look at me.

"Noah, be quiet," I say through clenched teeth. I'm trying not to cry over this bullshit with Liam and Noah, I am. I'm trying to be strong and hold my ground. He's been gone for ten years and he can't just show up here and act like nothing is wrong.

"What's going on?" Nick asks in his quiet and calming doctor tone. It's driving me nuts. I want him to tell Noah that he can't talk to Liam. I need him to back me up on this, but he doesn't. He just starts the car and backs out of the parking lot.

"You going to talk to me?" he asks. I shake my head, staring out the window at the passing store fronts. Merchants are out decorating for the fall and I realize I haven't. I need to. I can't be lacking when my store is prominent on Main Street.

"Drop me off at the shop please," I ask without looking at Nick. He reaches for my hand. I let him hold it, but don't hold his. I'm too pissed and the last thing I want is to be coddled.

"Josie –"

"Don't Josie me. I need to go to work. I should've never taken the day off." Nick doesn't respond, he just nods and drives toward my shop. When he pulls up to the curb I jump out without saying goodbye. I know I'll regret my attitude later, but right now I'm pissed that no one is on my side.

The fragrant smell of flowers over-powers me when I open the door. I forgot to leave the fan on when I left the other night and wonder how many flowers are ruined as a result. Ruined by everything that is Liam because he showed up here, in my shop, my one place that has nothing to do with him and now it's tainted.

I turn on only the back light, hoping to avoid people coming in. Regardless of the sign saying Closed, locals will still come in and visit. They like to talk, drink coffee and tell me their life stories while I trim and prepare bouquets.

The crunching of glass reminds me of Liam again. It seems that no matter where I turn, he's there interrupting my life, creating havoc in his path. Who knew his return would cause me so much turmoil.

Even Katelyn has opened her arms to him like the last ten years haven't mattered. Nick only wants him to sign away his rights and Noah... Noah wants Liam to be his best friend. And I want... I don't know what I want except for everything to go back to the way it was two weeks ago when Mason was walking in here on Monday morning ordering flowers for his wife.

Once the glass is cleaned, I turn on my iPod and get to work starting on my window displays, to create the perfect fall image, lining my window with mums and corn stalk. I'll have to remember to ask Noah, if he's talking to me, if he can make me a scarecrow. I add bushels of dried lavender to give the window just a bit more color. Not everything has to be red and gold.

Propping the door open for fresh air, I decide the steps need mums and cornstalks too. I need to keep busy or I'm going to start thinking about Liam and Noah and Nick. I stop dead in my tracks. How can Liam come to my mind over Nick when he's been there since Noah was three? How does he become third in my thought process?

It's simple, he shouldn't. He's so much more of a man than Liam. He's smart and educated, accelerating through college to open his small practice to give back to the community. He's the type of man someone thinks about first, not last.

"Need some help?" I don't turn around because I know that voice. I'll never forget that voice whether he's yelling or whispering into my ear. It's the same one that haunts my dreams, turning them into nightmares lately.

"I don't need anything from you, Liam." I tie the last of the stalks into the metal hooks on the façade. They'll hold as long as we don't have some freak wind storm.

But then again, Liam did blow into town without any warning.

"I just want to talk, Josie. We can be adults about this."

The moment I turn around I wish I hadn't. For the first time, I'm really looking at him, all of him. His arms are bare and I can finally see his tattoos – not that I was trying to earlier but I've been curious. I focus on them before granting my eyes permission to take in the rest of him. His arms are still defined, just like in high school, but probably more now. His jeans, distressed and likely expensive, not the Levi's he wore when we dated, hang loose on his waist.

Even with a belt they look as if they might fall down if he isn't careful.

He looks at me when my eyes reach his and smirks, but not with the smug intent from before. He knows I'm checking him out and he's allowing me to do so without calling me out on my bullshit.

I've never thought tattoos were sexy, but staring at Liam now I wonder if he has any that I can't see and I want to ask him what they all mean.

"Do you have...?" I trail off. That question is crossing a line that I'm not willing to step over.

"Do I what?"

"Nothing, never mind," I say shaking my head. I walk up the stairs and leave him standing on the sidewalk. I kick the door shut, effectively shutting him out.

"Josie," he says so softly I almost allow my heart to break. I miss that voice and now its here, banging in my head. I just want to scream and tell it to move out.

"I'm sorry for earlier and I wanted to ask you about something you said."

I push my hands into my hair while he speaks to my back. When he touches me, I want to melt and crawl into his arms, but that is the old me. This me turns and looks at him with nothing but anger and hatred in my eyes and he knows it because he steps back and shakes his head.

I raise my eyebrow indicating he can continue.

He takes a deep breath and looks at me before staring at the ground. He plays with his lip and I fight every urge I have to take his hand away from this mouth and lock his fingers with mine, just like I used to.

"You said you tried to tell me about Noah. I know I changed my number and that was a shit thing to do, but you said you tried and I'd like to know how."

"Why should I tell you?" I cross my arms over my chest defiantly.

"I'm asking you to give me a chance here, Jojo. I know I screwed up, but you weren't fucking there so you don't have a clue what I was going through." Liam starts pacing and pulling at what little hair he has. "The stress and being alone, I just—"

"Cheated?" I interrupt.

His head snaps up in my direction and I know the answer before he even has to say the words. "Never," he whispers. "I would've never disrespected you like that. When we were together I never even looked at another girl the way I looked at you."

"You left me. I obviously wasn't enough for you."

"My God, are even you listening to yourself? It wasn't about you. It was about me and this change I went through."

"I would have thought you could have come up with something better than that, given that you are such a genius with words. Why didn't you just tell me you weren't happy?"

"Because it wasn't like that, I felt like... like I was suffocating."

I didn't want to tell her like this because I knew I wouldn't be able to handle the picture in front of me. Her eyes drop, she steps back and her chest starts moving in and out as she tries to catch her breath. My heart breaks at this sight, worse than the night when I broke up with her. That night I took the coward route.

"I'm glad you're here, you must be tired." Her hand finds mine, she tries to pull me into her dorm room but I'm not budging.

"You don't want to come in?"

I do, but I can't. If I go in I'll never leave and nothing will change. My life will be the same pattern over and over again and if I don't change it I'm going to go nuts.

I shake my head just slightly but it's enough to peak her attention. "Something wrong, Liam?"

My throat starts to close, my heart... it feels like it's about to burst out of my chest. I know I'm doing the right thing, but why does it feel so horrible.

"I dropped out of school."

The first look of what is about to be a hissy fit spreads

across her face. I deviated from the plan. The all-American plan where I become an NFL football player and we live in a quiet neighborhood raising our two children, a boy and a girl, and she travels to my games and never misses one because she's my personal cheerleader.

"Okay, why?"

"I... um... I can't—"

"Can't what? You're scaring me, baby. Come in and we'll talk about it. We'll call your coach and fix this."

I feel a sense of relief wash over me when she says we'll call my coach. That is exactly what I don't want and I know I've made the right decision. I don't want to play football anymore.

"I can't be with you anymore, Josephine." I don't look at her when I say these words. I turn and walk away, ignoring her voice as she calls my name. I run down the hall, zigzagging through the people that just witnessed my girl and I break up.

I want to step forward and wrap her in my arms and tell her that night I made the biggest mistake of my life when I left her there. I should've busted in and packed her bags and taken her with me. The two day drive to Los Angeles would've been so much better with her curled up in my arms at night while we slept in the bed of the truck. My breakfast of Doritos and Coke would've been the best one I ever had because she would've shared it with me.

But instead I spent two days driving with tears streaking down my face because I did the most horrible thing I had ever done. I broke my own heart when I told her I was done.

"Jojo—"

She puts her hand up and I stop talking. When she looks up, it's that night all over again. Her make-up is running down her face, black and heavy, leaving a path of pain ruining her beauty.

"What was so important that you just left me?"

I sigh. I'm not sure how to explain Betty and the day that changed my life.

"I told you, I needed something different."

"It wasn't me?"

"No." I shake my head to emphasis my point. "It wasn't you. It was never you. I hate myself for not taking you with me. I should've, but I didn't think you'd go and I didn't want you to tell me no."

"So, you just break my heart and leave me to raise a baby by myself?"

"God damn it, Jojo. If I knew about the baby I would've stayed and figured something out. I would've married you and gone back to school."

"But you wouldn't have been happy?"

I can't answer her and she knows that. My silence is enough.

Josie takes a deep breath and nods. "So you went to California and became this big-time musician. You know what the funny thing is? I didn't think you liked the guitar that much. I know you would play while singing to me, but I thought you were always kidding. That sort of makes me a shitty girlfriend."

"You didn't think I was good?"

She shakes her head. "No, it's not that. I just thought it was a joke to you, something you did to irritate your dad."

"I always played. It made me calm and helped me express what I was feeling. When I went off to college, I played more and more. I went to an open mic night on campus and played. I loved it, loved every damn second of it and I tried to tell you, but you weren't listening. You just wanted to talk about football and your classes and how Mason and Katelyn were doing. You wouldn't listen to me when I tried to tell you my head was going to explode and that I woke up each night with my heart racing because I was so freaking lonely and hated school. My three best friends were at a different school and I was states away with no one."

Josie leans against the counter, watching me. It's the first time that she's actually looked at me and not had a scowl on her face. Her tear-streaked face is beautiful. I want to wipe away her tears. I want to take the last ten years and erase them.

I want to start over.

"Look I just came here to discuss Noah, but we got a little off track and I hate to see you cry."

"You do?" she looks up as if this is some joke for me.

I can't help but smile at how innocent she looks. "Just because I left that night doesn't mean things changed for me."

Surprise rolls over her face. She stares at me, probably wondering if I'm telling the truth. I am, but that is as close as I'm going to get to admitting it.

"I have a gig down at Ralph's, so I better get going. I'll see ya later, Jojo." I hesitate before turning away. I'd give anything to feel her arms around me, to hear her tell me to kick ass just one more time. To have her lips touch mine, even if it's only for a moment. It would be enough to last me another ten years.

THE PARKING LOT is full when I arrive at Ralph's. We ran into each other the night at the store and he asked me to do him a favor. I couldn't really say no since he used buy our beer for us. Besides, what's a little pub time gig amongst friends?

With my guitar strapped on my back, I throw open the door. The crowd is small and perfect. Ralph sees me and comes around the bar to encase me in his large arms.

"Thank you so much, Liam." He pats me on the back. His grin is thanks enough.

"Anything for you, but uh, didn't you advertise?"

"Yeah, I did," he says scratching his head. "But everyone thought I was jerking their chains."

I start laughing. That's the funniest shit I've heard in a long time. "It's good. We'll have a good time."

I follow Ralph to the bar and enjoy a few legal beers with him for the first time ever. People mill around, ignoring me and I like it. A few stop by and say hi, but they're talking to Liam Westbury, not Page.

Ralph tells me that he found himself a missus and that he's all domesticated now. I find that hard to believe but congratulate him. He invites me over for dinner and it hits me that my time here is almost over. I tell him maybe some other time because I've got to head back on Monday. His face is pensive, but he tells me he understands with me being a big time musician and all.

I wish I understood.

I finally take to the small stage. Me, my guitar, a stool and a bottle of Bud. There aren't lights shining in my face. No screaming girls throwing their underwear at me. My band is not behind me complaining about the sound and when I look off to the left of the stage there is no one standing waiting for me to put on the perfect show.

It's just me, in a pub with a hundred people or so.

Ralph dims the lights and I see a few cameras come out. The flash blinds me, but I'm used to it.

"So, I'm Liam Page." The crowd was quiet until I spoke. A few of the patrons cat call, others whistle and this reminds me why I get up on stage night after night. I love this feeling. I love the moment when my finger strums my guitar for the first chord on a song that I wrote and the crowd goes wild. I love looking out and seeing people sing my songs as if they were their own.

As I play, people pair off and dance. This is the first time in years that I've done a solo set in a pub and I remember why I like it so much. The fans are involved; they're part of the show. The longer my set, the more show up. Ralph is doing a great business tonight and is keeping me supplied with a steady amount of beer even though he's taking away half-empty bottles.

Someone yells that she loves me; I say 'thanks'. Never will I or have I told fans that I love them, even with something as innocent as this. I've only loved one person in my life and those words are saved for my girl and now my son.

Sitting up here I realize I want to be a dad to Noah. I want him to see me like this and know there's more to life than just football. He can be an artist, a musician or even live under a bridge and I'd still support his decision, if he'll let me.

When I look up, Ralph is hugging someone and standing next to them is the red head I saw Josie with at her shop the other day. When Ralph moves back, it's Josie that he's hugging. She stays in the back, I can barely make her out in the darkness, but I can feel her. She lives in my skin.

"This song, I just wrote it so you guys are the first ones to hear it. I apologize if it's a little rough."

I look out, hoping she'll show her face to me. I sing the

first verse in her direction, my eyes trained on the last location that I saw her. My second verse rips through me, opening so many wounds.

> "Arms of a stranger, a warm blooded kiss,
>   trying to fill the void, of the one that
>   I miss.
> Perfume whispers, lashes and lace, but I can
>   only hear your voice, I'm so out of place.
> All these painkillers, that's all they are.
> Painkillers."

I finish the last riff, unable to look at the back of the room to see if she's still standing there. This song was for her, a way for me to tell her without having to say the words what I am without her.

16

JOSIE

I went to see Liam sing at the pub two nights ago. Two nights, but I haven't been able to stop thinking about him. Listening to him sing, even if the words were telling me about his life, made me want to rush the stage and pull him tight in my arms, but the song wasn't for me. He was performing for his fans, giving them the Liam Page that they love. On that stage, that wasn't my Liam. He was someone I don't know.

I did the unthinkable after seeing him play; I downloaded his albums and listened to them straight through. Some songs made my cry, some made me laugh, a few of them made me so angry. Listening to him sing about lost love, the love that he threw away like it meant nothing. He had no right telling the world about us. It's like he was telling me he's sorry without having to look me in the face.

I'll see him today and I don't know what to say or how to act. Do I pretend that I wasn't at his show on Friday, act like I don't care or will he know? Did Ralph tell him? I'm confident that he didn't see me since I stayed in the back with

Jenna. We listened to two songs before I had had enough and needed to leave.

I couldn't watch him up there. I couldn't pretend that he didn't affect me. And worst of all, Jenna knew. She looked at me with such sad eyes and held my hand as we walked out of the pub. She didn't ask, all she said was Noah's name and I broke down.

I miss Liam and I don't want to. I'm with Nick. He loves me. We're going to get married and maybe have a baby together. That's the plan. We live together, even though I never asked him to move in. He sort of stopped staying at his own place. We didn't discuss it. I was afraid if I said something he'd leave me like Liam did.

So why is my heart telling me to give Liam a chance?

I rest my head on the window as we drive to Katelyn's. She asked that we all come over and treat this Sunday the same as we always have. Last week we didn't watch football, we mourned. Honestly I'm in no mood to celebrate with stupid touchdown dances and cocktail weenies.

Nick drives with one hand and slips his other into mine, his thumb caressing mine. For a fleeting moment I remember what it was like when Liam held my hand.

Yesterday, Liam Westbury, asked me to Homecoming. He said he'd call me last night, but he didn't. I'm prepared for him to tell me he's joking or that he decided to go with Candy Appleton because she'll put out. I mean that's what boys want, right? They're looking for something easy so they can say they did it.

Well, I'm not going to do it with Liam Westbury so if that's why he asked me, he's got another thing coming.

I take deep, calming breaths. I'm going to be late for homeroom but I don't care. Liam is in there and I don't really want to see him right now. My mom was right; a boy like Liam Westbury wants nothing to do with a girl like me. I'm from the wrong side of Beaumont.

I slam my locker shut and turn, smashing right into a wall of body. I step back and look up. Liam's peering down at me, his eyes full of life. He pulls my hand into his and leads us to the double doors. I'm no longer going to be late. I'm officially skipping my first class so Liam can break my heart. At least I technically only had half a day to get used to the idea of dancing with him.

Liam pushes the heavy metal doors open, his grip on my hand tightening. He takes us to the football field. Oh god, he wants to make out under the bleachers. Do I want this? If I don't, maybe he'll tell me he can't go to the dance with me. I wish I had talked to Katelyn about this before she ran off with Mason. I know they are close to doing it. She talks about it all the time, but I don't think I want to do it just yet.

We bypass the football field and head toward the baseball field. He wants to do it in the dugout. I guess that's better than behind the bleachers because at least there's a bench I can lay on.

He pulls us around the back of the dugout, away from view of the school. I know what he wants now. I look down and wonder if I'll get grass stains on my knees.

His free hand cups my face and I guess I should be happy he wants to at least kiss me first, or maybe this is some type of tongue test. Oh, how I wish I could call Katelyn right now.

"Why are you hiding?"

I shake my head, pushing my face into his hand more. He's still holding my other hand, probably trying to prevent me from leaving.

"You're too beautiful to hide, Josie."

"I'm not ready," I blurt out. *I cover my mouth as my eyes go wide. He's confused by my outburst and shakes his head.*

"I just want to talk," he says. *"I'm sorry for not calling last night, my father was on my case and by the time he was done and I finished my homework it was after nine and I didn't want to disturb your parents if they were sleeping."*

I think I'm in love.

"If I knew all I had to do was hold your hand to make you smile, I would've done this yesterday." I didn't mean to smile but thinking about how awkward I was with Liam, I can't help it. He was so understanding and caring.

I sit up straight and give Nick my best reassuring smile. I'm not going to be able to blame my mood on Mason for much longer. Sooner or later he's going to start asking questions.

Questions that lead to answers that I'm not ready to hear or accept.

When we pull into Katelyn's driveway, Liam's motorcycle sits in the carport. I close my eyes and wonder what it would be like to get on the back, to lean forward and press my chest against him and wrap my arms around his waist.

A knock on the window startles me. "You comin' in?" Nick asks before I can open the door. When I step out, he pulls my hand into his. "Are you okay?"

"Yeah, I'm fine," I say as I lead us into the house.

I'm not prepared for what I find inside. Noah runs past me, my son who hasn't spoken to me since Friday, right up to Liam and shows him his Sports Illustrated. The sight of Liam sitting there on the couch, dressed in a football jersey with Peyton next him, and my son standing there eager to show him something in a magazine is nothing compared to Liam leaning forward and forgetting about the game just so he can talk to Noah.

I run off to the bathroom before Nick can see my tears. I'm not being fair to him. Never have I complained about Liam not being in Noah's life and now that he's here, I want it. I want to see Noah happy and be able to say he has a dad, but I also know Nick wants that title. He might deserve the role, but maybe I owe Liam the opportunity to let Noah make that choice.

When I come back to the living room, the scene is comical. Liam has all the kids around him and Nick is sitting by himself. I try not to laugh as I take a seat next to Nick. Liam watches me out of the corner of his eye and smirks when Nick puts his arm around me. He full out smiles when he sees Nick pulling me close and I know Nick is wondering why I'm rigid and didn't just fall into the crook of his arm.

"Well, I hate to break up this party, but I promised Miss Peyton we'd watch at least one game downstairs," Liam says causing Peyton to jump and Noah's face to fall. Liam leans over and whispers something into Noah's ear and he smiles.

Seeing Noah's face light-up, I realize that I need to put my anger aside and do what's right for my son and give Liam a chance. My decision will hurt Nick, but it's something that I need to do for Noah.

P eyton and I watch an action-packed game that goes into overtime. I still can't get over the fact she knows the calls better than half of the officials. She has me cracking up; she's extremely vocal and holds her position well.

"Are you going to play football?" I ask her, curious whether this is something she and Mason discussed.

"Well, I'm not going to be a cheerleader like my mama was."

Her response effectively shuts my mouth. Mason loved having Katelyn on the sidelines for his games and I admit it was sweet pleasure having my girl cheer for me. The best part was the away games. The cheerleaders would ride back with us. Josie and I always sat in back where it was darkest. My lips never left a part of her body until we pulled into the school parking lot.

Elle comes down, dressed the exact opposite of her sister. These girls are a spitting image of their parents.

"Mommy says it's time for lunch." She turns and runs up the stairs, not waiting for an answer.

"What do you think? Should we head up for some grub?"

Peyton climbs onto my back. I hoist her up and run around their basement like a crazed man just so I can listen to her laugh.

"Can we do this again next Sunday?"

I stop running and pull her around to rest on my hip. "I gotta head back to work, but maybe we can watch the game together on the computer."

"I don't have a computer." I'm not going to let that stop me. I kiss her cheek and tell her not to worry about it.

When we get upstairs, everyone has congregated in the living room for lunch. Katelyn made just about every football food known to man. Peyton and I fix our plates and join everyone for the next game.

Noah's sitting on the floor so I sit down next to him. I notice that he smiles, but I'm not going to call attention to it. I told him after I watched the game with Peyton we'd go out back and work on his pass route timing. I'd like to find a way to prolong my day with him, but I know Josie isn't going to let me. I still need to sit down and talk to her about Noah and some type of visitation. Maybe we start with phone calls every few nights and I can come back to see him every month.

More importantly we need to tell him that I'm his dad, whether Josie wants to or not. I can imagine he's going to be hurt and probably hate my guts, but I'll do whatever I can to make it up to him. Not being a part of his life is not an option for me.

Noah's plate is empty, so I take mine and his into the kitchen to throw them away. Josie comes in behind me, her perfume weaving its way into my senses. I hate that she can smell so fucking good at Sunday football and I can't touch her.

"Hey," she says, shocking me. I thought for sure we were playing the avoidance game.

"Hi," I reply, barely looking at her. I pretend to clean, the ultimate chick move in avoiding an awkward conversation.

She just stares at me, her hands pulling desperately at her belt loops. I can't stand here and look at her so I call for Noah and ask if he's ready to go outside. He runs up to me, football in hand and races me to the door. I take one last look at her, her head down, teeth pushing a deep dent in her bottom lip, before heading outside.

I teach Noah everything I know. I'm surprised I even remember half of this shit, but it all comes back to me with each question he asks. I realize how lucky Nick is, living the life that should've been mine. He's got my girl and my boy and there isn't jack shit I can do about it except watch from the sidelines.

"Can you come to my game on Friday?" Noah asks with such hope in his voice. Just looking at him tears my heart into pieces.

"Let's go sit down," I say as I set my hand on his shoulder and bring him over to the picnic bench. "You know that I live in Los Angeles, right?" Noah nods. "Well I have to go back to work, I have deadlines and people are depending on me. I was supposed to just be here for the funeral and leave the next day, but then I met you and I really like hanging out with you and Peyton asked me to watch football so I stayed. I tell myself I'm leaving tomorrow and I need to do something first, but then I gotta head back to my cat, ya know, because he misses me."

"But he hates you."

"Yeah, buddy he does." I start to laugh, Noah joins in. When his blue eyes look up at me, I know I need to make this right. "I'm kinda hoping I can talk to your mom and maybe we can talk on the phone or something."

"She'll say no. She hates you or something, says I'm not supposed to talk to you. I did today because she won't yell in front of Katelyn."

Listening to my son tell me that my girl – his mother – hates me really doesn't sit well with me.

I need to fix it.

"I'll talk to your mom okay? Just don't be hard on her. She lost her friend and sometimes memories are hard to deal with."

He nods and when he looks at me, a piece of me dies. I don't want to leave him even if he never knows I'm his dad. I want to be his friend.

We both look up when the sliding glass door opens. Josie steps out with her arms wrapped around her body. Her eyes are red, she's been crying. I want to ask her why, but I also don't want to care. I should, but I can't. She has Nick and I need to accept that.

"I guess it's time for you to go," I say to Noah who looks like he's about to throw the football at his mom.

"Actually," she says as she steps closer. "I was wondering if you wanted to have dinner with me and Noah tomorrow at our house."

I look past her, into the living room where Nick is talking animatedly with Katelyn. "No thanks," I say much to Noah's chagrin. I hold my hand up for him to stop. "I'm not a fan of Nick's. I'm not sure I can make it through dinner with him."

Josie turns and looks into the house and when she turns

around she's shaking her head. "Nick is going away tomorrow for a conference. It will just be me and Noah."

No Nick. My girl, my son and me? Sign me up.

"What time?"

"How about five-thirty? I close the shop at five and walk home—"

"I'll pick you up," I say before really thinking about it. I only have the Ducati and one helmet. Guess I'm shopping for that tomorrow. Josie tries to hide her elation but her face tells me everything I need to know; she's fantasized about being on the bike with me and I'm about to make her fantasy come true.

"So I guess I'll see you," I say to Noah. This makes him smile.

I get up and walk the few steps to Josie. I'm closer than I should be, especially with Nick inside the house. I lean in, my lips grazing her cheek. "You'll love the ride, I promise," I whisper into her ear. As much as I want to see her expression, touching her has killed me. I move away as quickly as I can and back into the house.

I fire up my bike, revving the engine so she gets an idea of what she's in for tomorrow and take off. Her scent lingers on my skin, filling my helmet. I'm not sure how I'll handle Josie on the back of my bike tomorrow, but it will be my five minutes of paradise.

18

JOSIE

My palms are sweating.

I'm watching the clock.

The minute hand is moving ungodly slow.
Every tick echo's throughout the shop. I sent Jenna home
early because she kept laughing at me and none of this is
funny. I would've called and told him that I'd walk home
but I don't have his number and it's not like I can call directory assistance for Liam Page's freaking number.

They'd laugh at me just like Jenna has all day. Except
they would probably cackle because directory service is
usually old women who have nothing better to do except
give people like me a hard time when you ask for something
totally and completely stupid.

Oh god. This is like high school all over again.

Every time I heard a motorcycle outside I ran to the
window and when Jenna snickered I pretended to
straighten something out. I hate her today.

I wipe my hands on my jeans for the millionth time. He
should be here any moment and I'll tell him I can't ride with
him because I have no helmet and those are required and

even if they weren't I wouldn't get on that death trap. He might kill me for keeping Noah from him. I mean that seems logical, right?

The door chimes and before I can turn and greet the customer, I smell his cologne. I take a deep breath before turning around. I don't know why but this feels like a date when it's so not a date. I mean I'm engaged to another man and we're going to get married and I can't date Liam regardless of our history. I need to turn off my brain.

When I finally lay my eyes on him, he's delicious, all six feet of him. He's not wearing the black leather jacket I've grown accustomed to and once again I find myself staring at his arms. My mind wanders up his left arm and then his right. My fingers want to reach out and trace the ink. My heart wants to know if they hurt, if he wants more.

He's allowing me to stare at him, drink him in and I think I realize that this might be the last time I see him. He may not want to tell Noah that he's his dad. Hell, he may not want to even know Noah past this trip. I'm not sure I want that.

"Are you ready, Jojo?" My heart soars and it shouldn't. I should tell him not to call me that, but I don't. He's watching my every move, waiting for me to freak out on him.

"I can walk," I mumble.

Liam rolls his eyes and shakes his head. When he reaches for my hand I let him take it. As soon as he touches me, it's like a thousand butterflies fluttering over my skin. I haven't felt this way in years. I take two steps toward him, leaving just a small space between us. In a few short minutes I'll be touching him and I may not want to stop.

My mind is foggy, but I need to keep my senses clear. I remind myself that I'm an engaged woman. The man before me, this sexy beautiful man who is taking my hand in his like he's done so many times before, is the same man that broke my heart.

He lets go of my hand as soon as we're outside. I want to reach for him, but I know it's not the right thing to do. He holds a helmet in his hand and smiles when he shows it to me.

"I got this for you," he says before slipping it over my head. He's still smiling when he fixes my hair on the outside. I'm smiling too, but he can't see me. "Where do you live?"

I give him my address and watch as he swings his leg over and straddles his bike. "Put your hand on my shoulder and bring your leg over." I do as he says. Once I'm situated he puts on his helmet and starts his bike. The vibration sends chills up my spine and I know now why women love a man with a motorcycle.

He reaches behind and pulls my hands forward, wrapping them around his torso. My front is pressed up against his back and this is just like I imagined it would be. I rest my chin, as much as I can, on his shoulder and I can feel his body relax before putting his bike into gear.

He drives down Main Street, maintaining the speed limit, taking each turn to my house with ease. I never thought I'd feel so safe on a motorcycle.

He pulls into the driveway and turns off the bike. He removes his helmet and helps me get off first. When I pull off my helmet he starts laughing and shaking his head.

"What the hell is your problem?" I ask as I start patting down my hair. This just proves why I should never wear a helmet.

"Nothing, I've just imagined you a million times sitting

behind me, but never did I imagine you'd flip your hair back and forth when you took off the helmet."

"You've imagined me on your bike?" I ask my voice barely above a whisper. He nods and puts the kickstand down so he can get off.

"You're the first girl I've ever let ride with me." He steps closer, his fingers move a strand of hair way from my face, curling it behind my ear. "The only one, Jojo." He steps away, giving me some much needed space. I need to understand what just happened.

He follows me into the house, through the door leading to the kitchen and dining room. He looks around, taking in my small home. Nick says we can move after we're married, but Noah and I have lived here since I left school. Not sure I want to move just yet.

Noah comes running out of his room and hugs Liam. I leave them to have their moment and move into the kitchen and start preparing dinner. I made most of it last night so Liam could spend as much time as possible with Noah.

"Noah, did you finish your homework?"

"No, can I finish it after Liam leaves?"

"Can I see your homework? Maybe I can help." Noah runs up to his room, his footsteps heavy and solid.

"Hey, Noah?" I yell.

"Yeah?"

"Why don't you play a game or something for a few minutes, I need to talk to Liam."

"Okay," he yells back. The TV turns on instantly, loud with some auto racing game.

"Thank you for this, Josie."

I smile and nod, not sure how to respond.

"I'm supposed to leave tomorrow, but Noah says he has a game on Friday and I really don't want to miss it."

I turn on the oven and place dinner inside to heat up. I motion for Liam to sit at the table. He pulls out my chair for me, something Nick has never done. I sit down, clasping my hands in front of me.

"Did you really not know?" I ask. I hate asking, but I need to know. Liam shakes his head, his eyes focusing on something... anything but me. When he meets my eyes, I can see the pain, he's telling the truth.

"I found your agent or whatever and called," I start, hating that I have to relive this time of my life. A time when I felt so desperate to reach him, when I needed him the most and he wasn't there. "I left message after message until someone finally called back and said that you told them that you didn't know me."

Liam reaches for my hand. He pulls it to his forehead. "I didn't know. I would've come home and done things the right way."

"Noah doesn't know. He knows that Nick isn't his dad, but sometimes it's just easier for him to tell people that he is. I don't want him hurt, Liam and I'm afraid that if I let this happen you'll disappear tomorrow."

"I won't. I know my word is shit to you, but I'll do anything to prove it. I want to be his dad. He's supposed to be ours, Jojo, and I fucked that up."

I can't keep the tears at bay when he says things like this. No wonder he's a freaking song writer and makes millions of women fall in love with his music.

"We can tell him tonight, if you want—"

"I want to, but—"

"No, Liam, no buts. I just told you I don't want him hurt."

"It's not like that. I have to go back to L.A. and I was going to leave tomorrow, but he asked me to come to his game so I cleared my schedule for the week so I can stay and see him play. I'll have to go back for work, but once he knows, I can come back once a month to see him. We can figure out the rest from there."

I knew his lifestyle would dictate how much of a dad he was going to be. I'm not sure if I thought he'd move back here or not.

"I know," I say softly. I want to say what about me, but I have Nick and he's been really great to me and Noah. "I'll go get Noah so he can start hating me." Liam reaches for my hand, pulling me back down.

"He won't hate you; I won't allow it." I nod and release his hand. I take a moment to compose myself before calling for Noah. He comes thundering down with a smile on his face. He looks just like Liam when he smiles.

Liam looks up when we walk into the room. If I didn't know better I'd think that he'd been crying. We sit down, Noah in between us. He looks at Liam, then me, smiling.

"We've got something to tell you."

19

LIAM

"Okay," Noah says. I can feel his leg start to swing under the table. Reaching down, I set my hand on his knee, calming his jitters. Josie shifts in the chair, leaning closer to Noah. I do the same thing, although I'm not sure why. I look at her and raise my eyebrow. We didn't discuss who was going to tell him. I think it should be her. I can't see myself blurting out that I'm his dad. My luck it would come out like Darth Vader – minus the respiratory issues.

Josie clears her throat and smiles at Noah. "Remember when you asked me if Liam was my boyfriend?" Noah nods, his leg starts up again. I realize I'm not going to be able to keep him calm. Hell, I'm not even calm. I just have years of practice in stoicism.

"Well, Liam and I dated for a long time in high school and then he went away to college and things didn't work out for us, but..." Josie stops and clears her throat. I know this must be hard for her, remembering how good we had things until I screwed everything up. "I'm sorry I didn't tell you sooner, sweetie."

"Tell me what?" Noah breaks in. His eyes are drawn in. I can tell he doesn't like to see his mom cry. He puts his hand on her shoulder and rubs it.

"Liam is your dad, baby." Josie sobs. My leg slams into the table as I get up, rushing to her side. I fall to my knees, pulling her into my arms. Her tears wet my neck, her cries muffled. I know I shouldn't, but I have to. I kiss below her ear, her cheek.

"Everything will be all right. I won't leave. I promise," I whisper with each kiss. She brings her face up, her eyes wet, red and puffy. My hands cup her face, pulling her closer. I kiss her full on lips. Lips I've missed for so long. When she starts to pull away, I want to hang on, but she's not mine and I shouldn't have kissed her, not like that.

"I'm sorry," I say. She nods and wipes her face with the back of her hands. I move back to my seat without looking at Noah. He just saw a man kiss his mom.

A man she's not engaged to.

I risk a look at Noah, he's smiling. I'm not sure why, but he looks like a kid in a candy store.

"I'm sorry I didn't tell you when you asked before," Josie says. Her fingers thread through his hair which seems to relax his jittery leg.

Noah shrugs. "I already knew."

Josie and I look at each other, stone faced. Our heads both turn slightly as we look at Noah. "What do you mean you knew?" I ask.

"Remember that day in the museum?" I nod. "Well I was looking at a picture of you and Mason and a teacher said I looked just like you and then I saw you in the bathroom and when I said my mom's name you looked at me kinda funny. So I just guessed it."

"You didn't want to say something?" I ask.

"I didn't know if you liked me or if you wanted to be my dad."

Looking at my son with tears in my eyes I see me at this age. I reach out, cupping his face with my hand. "Hell yes I want to be your dad. My god, Noah, since the day I saw you, I've been bugging your mom about meeting you."

"Was I an accident like Junior Appleton?"

"No," I answer before Josie can say anything. Her eyes go wide. "Your mom and I talked about having kids all the time. I was going to marry her, buy her a nice fancy house and we were going to have a family."

Noah looks at Josie who nods in agreement. When he looks back at me, his eyes are like daggers. "What happened?"

"I went to college and some things changed. Instead of taking your mom with me, I left everyone I knew behind and went to California to try something different. I didn't know about you until I met you the other day. Your mom," I look up at Josie and smile. "She loves you and she tried to find me, so don't be angry at her okay?"

"Okay."

"Remember when I said I had to go back to work. I'm going to stay for this week's game, then head back. But I'll be back and you can call me anytime you want to talk or have a question about football."

"Can I tell people you're my dad?"

I look to Josie for approval. She shrugs her shoulders. I think that Beaumont is far enough off the beaten path that paparazzi won't bug him, but I'm not sure. I also don't want him to feel like he has to hide me.

"You can, but listen, buddy. There are people who like to take my picture and think they can get close to me through my friends. If anyone gives you a hard time or starts following you around, you just call me and I'll take care of everything, okay?"

"And we need to tell Nick," Josie says as she runs her hand through Noah's hair. I thought she had which would explain why he was so angry yesterday. I know I shouldn't care, but he's been raising my son. I should respect his feelings.

"Listen to me, Noah. I want you to listen to Nick and treat him the same because he's your dad too. You are going to be one of those special boys that have an amazing set of parents."

The timer on the stove goes off and Noah breathes a sigh of relief before announcing that he's starving to death. Josie jumps up and hurries into the kitchen, leaving Noah and I sitting at the table.

"Do you love my mom?"

"Yes," I reply without hesitation.

"Like really, really looooove her?"

"Where do you learn this stuff?" I don't remember knowing what love was at nine years old. My only focus was football and how far I could throw the ball. Girls weren't even on my radar at this age.

"School."

"What else do they teach you in school these days?"

Noah shrugs. "Do you love her like you did before?"

"Yes," I say again because it's the truth. I never stopped loving her and absence doesn't make the heart grow fonder. I've been in love with Josephine Preston since I can remember and now I'm too late. "But it doesn't change things. Your mom has moved on and is going to marry Nick. You and I, though, you're going to be my sidekick."

"Can I go on tour with you?"

Josie enters just as Noah asks. I'm not sure how to

answer but I'm sure as hell not telling him no. Josie is watching me out of the corner of her eye, waiting for me to screw this up. She sets plates in front of us and takes a seat across from Noah.

"Maybe," I say as I pick up my fork. "It will depend on where I'm going and if it's during the summer. You can't miss school and you don't want to miss football. Do you play any other sports?" I dig into my dinner and hum when the savory chicken hits my taste buds. I haven't had a home cooked meal in a long time. Even the food at Katelyn's was just party food. This is a real dinner.

"I play baseball because Nick likes it, but I want to learn the guitar."

"I'll teach you."

"You will? Awesome!"

Dinner conversation flows fairly well. We talk about his teacher and his homework. He tells us that he has a crush on a girl at school but doesn't want to give us her name. Josie and Noah ask about Los Angeles and what it's like. I tell them there are a lot of people, the traffic is horrible so I hate leaving my place and that it can be really hot. But we have Disneyland and nice beaches and the Hollywood sign.

Noah asks what my cat's name is and I'm ashamed to admit I never named it. Noah says that's why it hates me and he's probably right.

Noah drills me about music and MTV asking me if I like being on there and I tell him no, but that I don't have a choice. He says he listened to some of my music and tells me I'm really good. I wasn't prepared when he asked who my songs were about. I shrugged and went back to eating. There were some things I just wasn't going to answer.

Being a school night, our time is cut short. Noah complains, but I ask him if I can come watch his practice tomorrow. I remind him that I'll also be at his game this week. Josie invites me over for dinner again and I eagerly agree. I want to spend time with her simply because being in the same room as her calms me. It also spurs my creative side and I can't wait to get back in the studio, even though I'll be leaving them both behind.

Josie and I sit down for coffee once Noah is in bed and she sets some rules. I don't exactly agree, but understand where she's coming from. No elaborate gifts or fancy toys. I ask about a phone and she says yes, as long as I'm the one paying. I laugh and then quickly realize that maybe she and Nick aren't sharing expenses. The more I think about it the more pissed off I get. If he's living here and playing dad, why is she worrying about money? I put a note in my phone to write her a check for ten years of back child support.

Leaving Josie's house is hard. I hate the idea of them alone in the house by themselves, but she assured me she's used to it. I still don't like it.

Instead of going back to my hotel, I head for the cemetery. I haven't been back since we buried Mason, and I could really use him right now. Even if just means he's listening. I'm surprised I can find his plot in the dark, but I do. All his standing sprays are still in bloom and I wonder if Josie has been out here taking care of the flowers each day.

"So I have a son," I say while rearranging the flowers covering his plot. "I have a nine year old son who looks just like me and plays football. Quarterback no less. I'm guessing it's pretty cool being a dad. I don't know yet because I only found out by accident and Josie just told Noah today. He seems cool with it until he realizes I'm not around all time like Nick. God, how could you let her hook up with Nick Ashford? Man, when I saw him at your funeral I thought I was in the twilight zone. But I guess you guys became buddies or something, huh?"

I sit down in the dirt, pulling my knees to my chest. "I'm sorry, Mason. You'll never know how sorry I am for leaving like I did. I should've called or something, come home after a year. All I can say is that I'm sorry and I'll make it up to Katelyn and make sure she's taken care of. I can do that for her and you and your girls, especially Peyton. Someone is going to have to teach her a five step drop. Might as well be me."

I set my hand over his dirt pile and say a silent prayer before leaving. The ride back to my hotel is long and lonely. Now that I have Noah and he knows the truth, I want to spend all my time with him. I just need to figure out how.

20

JOSIE

I never thought I'd feel anything for Liam again. Those feelings had been long dead and then he started coming around. First it was dinner he brought over for Noah and me. He was already in the house and cooking when I came home from work. The next night I cooked again. He stayed late and when he pulled out my favorite movie and a bottle of wine, I knew I was I starting to lose it. I wanted more than anything to cuddle up next him on the couch, but he wouldn't sit next to me. He sat in the chair, looking uncomfortable while I sat on the couch as close to him as I could get.

The night Nick came home I half expected Liam to be in my kitchen, but he wasn't. I tried not to watch or listen for him to pull into my driveway, and knew deep down that he wasn't coming over. It didn't matter that I wanted to see him. He wasn't coming to see me anyway, just Noah, and I needed to accept that. Besides, I have Nick.

And Nick is who I want.

Nick is who I'm going marry.

Nick is the one who I've been with for the past six

years. We share a house and have been raising my son together.

So why am I sitting in the living room with the lights off, while he sleeps upstairs, going through my box full of Liam? I should be upstairs in bed with him, but since he's come home I've slept on the couch feigning a stomach ache. When Nick asked if I thought whether or not I was pregnant I wanted to cry. Not because I don't want another baby, but because if we have one, it won't look like Noah. It wouldn't look like me and Liam.

My finger trails over his football picture, his helmet tucked up underneath his arm. His eye black patches not showing his number, but Jo. His friends gave him such shit for that, but he didn't care.

"Hey beautiful." Liam picks me up. I can't help but squeal. I've officially turned into one of the girls I said I'd never be. Oh my god, I'm a cliché.

Liam puts me down, spinning me to face him. His eye black is different. His number is missing.

"You know you're wearing the name 'Jo' on your face?"

"Of course I know. It says Jojo."

"Yes it does," I laugh at how silly he is.

He pulls me closer, kissing me deeply. He's not afraid if we get caught by a teacher. I am, but he promises nothing bad will happen and I trust him.

"I love Jojo more than anything."

"You do, huh? Should I be worried?"

Liam shakes his head, a smirk breaking through his tough guy act. "You're my Jojo. Just mine," he says. He kisses me again before running off. He's halfway out to the field and I'm still watching his back side. He's got such a nice ass.

"Hey, Jojo?" he yells.

"Yeah," I yell back.

"I'm going to marry you someday."

I thought for sure we'd spend forever together. I thought our love was one of a kind. I would almost be okay if he had met someone else and fallen in love, but he didn't. He just left. He said he was suffocating.

I had this dream, the All-American dream, and we were living it, the head cheerleader dating the quarterback and captain of the football team. We were the poster kids for romance throughout the town. Everyone knew we were together and nothing was going to break us up. Other girls tried but Liam brushed them off so quick I felt sorry for them... sometimes.

We used to have dinner with his parents every Sunday night at the Beaumont Country Club. Mrs. Westbury was cold as ice and Mr. Westbury just looked down at me. I went to them when I couldn't get a hold of Liam, asking if they knew where he was, but his dad said he was happy that Liam finally put out the trash. I was so hurt that I blurted out that this trash is carrying his grandchild. "Well, the whore finally did it," he said before slamming the door in my face.

Liam hasn't asked about his parents and whether they know Noah. I don't know what he'll say if I tell him about his dad. I know deep in my heart Liam never thought I was trash.

Maybe he won't ask and I won't have to tell him.

Pressure on my shoulder wakes me. Squinting through one eye, I see Nick hovering over me. An immediate sense of dread washes over me when I open my eyes and see his expression. I sit up, pulling my afghan around me. Nick hands me a cup of coffee and sits down next to me.

"Aren't you going to be late for work?" I ask. I know I am, but Jenna can open the shop by herself.

"I called Barbara and told her I was going to be late. I thought we might need to talk." He points to the Liam box. The one I've been hiding for years. "It looks like you were taking a trip down memory lane."

I sip my coffee carefully while I think of what to say. I don't want to lie to him, but no matter what I say it will seem like a lie. Can you be in love with two different people? What if my feelings for Liam are only there because of Noah, because I'm finally getting to see my boy with his father? Is that the love I'm feeling for Liam?

"Mason—"

"It's not Mason that you were looking at, Josie. Please don't patronize me by lying." Nick won't look at me. We've never truly fought before. There've been many awkward moments especially after I told him 'no' each time he'd ask me to marry him.

"I'm sorry."

I set my cup down on the coffee table, careful not to use any of the pictures as a coaster. I try not to look at them as I pick them up, but one of Liam and I catches my eye. Nick's heavy sigh snaps me out of my reverie. I put the pile of pictures back in their safety box and shut the lid.

"Do you really need to keep those? You'll see most of those people at our reunion."

"Yes, I need to keep them," I snap.

"Really, why? So you can remember all the good times? Is that it?

"What do you want me to say, huh? That I'm sorry I kept those photos? I'm not sorry. He's my son's father, Nick, and whether you like it or not he's going to be around a lot more." I can't sit next to him anymore, I get up and start to pace. My hands are shaking I'm so angry.

"What the hell do you mean he'll be around more? Over

my dead body!" He stands, spilling his coffee. I'm so thankful I moved those pictures because they would've been ruined now.

"Why are we fighting about this? We knew this was going to happen one day. If Liam didn't come back, Noah was going to ask."

"Yeah, but I thought my fiancée would've at least talked to me first so we could make the right decision for our son."

I try not to roll my eyes at his usage of 'our son'. I know I'm being a bitch, but I did what's best for Noah. I go and retrieve a dish towel and start cleaning up the coffee.

"I made a decision. I invited Liam over for dinner and we told Noah the other night. I'm sorry I didn't consult you. I didn't do it to cause a fight. I thought I was doing the right thing."

"Right for who? You and Liam?"

"Right for Noah."

Nick paces in front of the living room window, his hands clenched together at the back of his neck. I walk over to him, placing my hand on his shoulder. He flinches and moves away from me.

"Did you sleep with him?"

"What? How can you ask me that?" I ask him incredulously. "I'm just... Really, Nick, after everything we've been through, how can you ask me that?"

"Simple," he says turning to face me. "I ask you over and over again to marry me and it's always 'no'. I asked after Mason passed away because I don't want to live like this anymore. Then Liam shows up. So maybe I'm thinking he's been in contact with you and you knew he was coming and you had this whole thing planned out."

"That's not fair."

"No, Josie, what's not fair is me coming home and

spending these past few nights in our bed alone only to wake and find you asleep on the couch with photos of your ex everywhere. Then you drop the bomb that you decided, by yourself, to tell a boy I've been raising, who his father is because you wanted to.

"This is not the Josephine I fell in love with. I don't know what happened while I was gone or what he's done to make you act like this, but I don't like it." Nick storms out of the house, slamming the door not only on me, but on our conversation.

AFTER NICK COMES home from work, we head to the field. Liam is leaving tonight after the game, so this is the last time he and Noah will see each other for a while. Liam bought him an iPhone and thought he'd be sneaky when he handed me a check for an obscene amount of money. I was told to keep it, if I didn't need it, use it for a rainy day or spend it on Noah however I wanted.

Nick's mood didn't improve once he saw Liam at the field. Noah ran up to him and jumped into his arms. I heard Nick mutter something unintelligible. I ignored him. I didn't go talk to Liam, but Peyton did. They stood together, she on his shoulders, and watched Noah play.

When it was over, Noah left the field and headed straight to Liam, infuriating Nick. I want Nick to be understanding. I get why he's not, but what's done is done. There's no going back. Noah's father is leaving and won't be back for who knows how long. Nick could at least give him a chance to say good-bye.

"Noah, let's go," Nick huffs as he throws the gear into the back of his truck. Liam shakes his head and walks over toward us, Noah right beside him. I can't believe how much they look alike.

"So, I'll be back next month for a week. As soon as I know which week I'll call and let you know, okay?" I nod, unable to find my voice. I don't want this reunion to end.

"You be good, okay? And listen to Nick just like we discussed." He bends down and hugs his son. The son he just met and is now leaving.

"Bye, dad," Noah says before running off to the truck. The look on Liam's face must match mine.

"Don't worry, Jojo," he whispers to me. He places a kiss on my cheek before walking way.

"Take care of my family, Nick," Liam says as he slips his helmet on muffling out Nick's tirade.

I watch Liam's bike as it flies down the road. When my eyes meet Nick's, he's glaring at me. He shakes his head, punching his truck in the process.

I think I just lost my fiancé.

21

LIAM

It feels good being back in my studio. Since returning, I've been writing like crazy. I think at this point I have enough for a new album. Today, my bassist, Jimmy, and drummer, Harrison, are coming in to lay down some melodies.

I should be happy, but I'm not. This is why I left my life behind. I'm antsy as fuck and want to get back to Beaumont. The first few days back were questionable. I tried to call Noah a couple of times but couldn't bring myself to do it. What if he didn't want to talk to me now that I was gone?

The moment I saw his face light up my screen, I knew that wasn't the case. When I answered he seemed happy, excited, asking a lot of questions about L.A. and the studio. He asked me to send him pictures of the cat and I did.

Now I can't talk to him enough. The hours that he's at school and the time difference make me anxious. Weekends are now my friend.

And I hate Mondays, effectively killing my high from spending hours chatting with my son. I haven't told the band yet, but I will. I just want to keep Noah to myself for a bit. Harrison is the only other parent around; he has a seven-year old boy. Quinn is a product of a one-night stand that turned into the baby mama dropping her blue bundle of joy on Harrison's door step. Instant daddy.

When I see Josie's face on my caller ID, panic ensues. Something must be wrong with Noah otherwise she wouldn't be calling. We haven't spoken since I left. It's not that I don't want to, but I don't want to screw shit up for her and Nick.

"Hello?"

"Hi." She's breathless. I close my eyes and count to ten. She can't talk to me like this. It kills me that she's not mine.

"Wha..." My voice catches in my throat from the way she said hi. I need to get a grip here. It was just a common two-letter word. It doesn't mean anything. "What's up?"

"Today is Monday." She says this like it's supposed to mean something to me. I rack my brain, wondering if Noah had mentioned something particular about this Monday.

"It usually follows Sunday," I say, hoping to lighten her mood.

"Mason sends Katelyn a dozen roses every Monday and today will be the first day that she won't get flowers since..." If I didn't know better I'd say she's crying.

"Well, we can't have Katelyn missing her flower delivery, now can we?" I pull up the internet and type in the address for the global florists. I choose a bouquet of lilies over the roses and request they be delivered via Josie's shop. "All set."

"What do you mean?"

"I mean I ordered her flowers. She'll get a delivery every Monday for a year."

"Liam..." her voice breaks and now I know she's trying to control her emotions. These past weeks have been hard on her. The Josie I knew was always strong and confident then she lost Mason and I returned, creating havoc. We stay on the phone for a few more minutes before she has to go and fill my order. Hanging up with her is the last thing I want to do, but work calls for both of us.

When the guys come in, they seem happy. This mini-vacation must've done them good. We sit down and I show them the songs I've been working on. Harrison starts laughing at a few of them, earning a punch from Jimmy. I sit stoically, waiting for them to say something.

"Did you fall in love while you were away?" Harrison asks. Yes, but I never really fell out of love. She just showed me what I've been missing all these years.

"No, saw a lot of old friends. My buddy died and left behind a wife and two kids. Sort of hits home, I guess."

"Well, I like them," Jimmy says. "Putting music down for these won't take us much time at all. I already have a few ideas."

We take to the studio and start brainstorming with different sounds. Most of the songs could end up being ballads, but we want to stay away from that. We need to add a rock vibe to keep our fans interested. If I put out an album full of love songs people will think I've gone soft.

"*Painkillers* has to be a slow song," I say when Jimmy starts singing it.

"Why? We could blow this one up."

I shake my head. "I want that one slow. I want people to feel the words and what they mean. I don't want them lost in the loud vibrations."

Painkillers is the first track we work on. It only takes a few tries before I'm happy with the melody. I'm going to have to push Sam to make this our first single. I want to release it as soon as possible.

After the guys leave for the night I work on mixing. Playing *Painkillers*, over and over, until I'm happy. I decide we're going to give it another shot tomorrow before we record the final.

Papers land on my mixing board. I turn down the track and leave my head phones on. I want to hear myself sing to Josie. This song has to be perfect. Sam is leaning against the board, pissing me off because she knows not to touch my shit. "What's this?"

"What do you want?"

"Were you going to tell me you're back in town?"

I turn away from her and move the papers she threw. "You're my manager, not my mother. You handle my affairs, not my personal life, Sam."

"Well, this is my job." She picks up the stacks of papers and starts flipping through them. "Let's see... 'Liam Page playing at Ralph's no cover.' 'OMG Liam Page is so hot he's at Ralph's free show.' Oh, and my personal favorite... 'Liam Page Debuts New Song at local pub.'"

"Get to the point. I'm busy."

"This!" She shakes the papers in my face. "Is my point! You were off doing god knows what with god knows who and decided to have a free show without even consulting me. Jesus, Liam! Do you know how much of a PR nightmare this is?"

I refuse to answer her because she'd never understand why I did the show in the first place. She doesn't do nice for any of her friends. It's all about what-can-you-do-for-me with her and that's not who I want to be. The show was a success and Ralph did a hell of a lot of business that night. I have no regrets.

"Are you listening to me?"

"Not really. I'm trying to work."

"I knew you heading back to that po-dunk town was a mistake. Maybe I should go check out Beaumont and see what all the excitement is about."

I pull off my head phones and stand-up to face her. "What's your problem?"

"You, Liam. I'm sick of this cat-and-mouse game we play. It's time to make a decision."

I start to laugh, anger building. "You're the one playing games. I'm not into you. What we did was a mistake, Sam, a very weak moment on my part because you were available and willing to give me what I wanted."

"You don't mean that," she whines. I stuff my hands into my pocket, feeling for my phone. It's time for me to call Noah. I walk away from her, until she grabs my arm. "Liam, what we had was special."

"What we had was sex, nothing more."

I leave her standing in the studio. I need to rein her in before she gets out of hand. Lately she's been more possessive and it's starting to scare me. I should've never mixed business with pleasure and she's strictly business.

I walk down the hall until I'm far enough away from the studio. Crouching down, I pull out my phone and call Noah.

"Hey dad," he answers before the first ring has completed. The sound of his voice sends warmth through my body. I want to record his voice so I can play it all the time.

"What's up, buddy? How was school?"

"It's okay. I have to do a history report, but mom said she'd help me."

"That's good. You know I'd help if I was there, right?"

"Yeah, I know." When he speaks, I know he means it. I

can't detect any remorse in his voice at all. "Can I ask you a question?"

"Of course." My knees start to cramp so I stand, leaning against the wall that holds my gold records.

"Do your mom and dad want to be my grandparents?"

I stiffen at the mention of my parents. I haven't spoken to them since the night I left. My dad told me I was a disgrace and stupid for giving up football to pursue music. Said I'd never make it. My mom just stood there, a tumbler of vodka in her hand.

"What are you doing home?"

You always know you're welcome in your home when you're greeted like that. Sterling folds and sets his newspaper down, pulling off his glasses. Bianca stands in the foyer, her vodka glass permanently stained with her scarlet red lipstick.

"I need to talk to you."

"What did you do, Liam? Are you in some type of trouble?"

"No, Sir. I..." I can't look at him. He's always looked down on me, making me feel two feet tall. "I left school."

"Obviously, you can return in the morning."

I shake my head. "I can't go back. I quit."

"What do you mean you quit?" he bellows causing my mom to jump, the ice rattling around in her glass.

"I thought it would be different and it's not and I've been talking to Grandma Betty—"

"YOU WHAT? Do you think I've raised you to be a Westbury so you can associate with trash like that?"

"Trash? She's your wife's mother," I point to mom who has no expression on her face. "My god, what is your problem? She's family. I know what you did. What you both did. Mom, you gave up your dreams to marry him." I point at my

dad. "And you made her. Why? Why weren't her dreams as important as yours? Look at her! She's a damn robot."

"Betty is clearly poison if that is what she told you. So tell me smart ass, what are your plans?"

"I'm going to go to Los Angeles for a bit to try my hand at music."

Sterling starts laughing. A maniacal laugh. Bianca walks into the room and fills her tumbler. She must coat her liver with medicine in order to function. Typical.

"If you do not return to school immediately, don't come back here."

"You're kicking me out for following a dream?"

Sterling picks up his paper and pops it open, crossing his leg. "No, Liam, I am simply instructing you of your options. You have two: you can go back to school, speak with your coach and secure your spot on the team, or you can walk out that door, lose your trust fund and forget that you're a Westbury."

"I don't know, buddy. Let's talk about it when I come back okay. My parents... they're difficult sometimes and we don't always get along."

"Okay. What are we going to do when you get here?"

"Well, I thought we could look for a house. I don't want to stay in a hotel when I'm there and I was thinking that maybe your mom will let you stay with me for the time I'm there, but I'll have to talk to her about it, okay? You don't need to bring it up. I'll take care of everything. I gotta go though so I'll talk to you tomorrow."

"Night, I love you dad."

"I love you too."

I slide down the wall after Noah hangs up. I knew my parents were going to come up sooner or later, I was just hoping for much, much later.

My hand runs through my hair. I think I'll grow it out to the way Josie liked it, maybe then she'll look at me with different eyes. I'm not going to lie, I want my girl back.

"Did you knock someone up?"

I turn to see Sam standing in the hall, hands on her hips. She's pissed.

22

JOSIE

With Halloween out of the way and the countdown to Liam's return looming, Nick is on edge. He hasn't changed much since Liam left last time and it's not like I haven't tried. He's uptight and stressed. He says its work, but I know it's me. It's my actions and disrespect for his feelings. I've put unnecessary strain on our relationship and haven't been fair to him.

I've thrown myself into work, as much as I can anyway. I've decided to expand and have rented out the adjacent building for more window frontage. I plan to add a coffee shop and bring in live music. When I showed Nick my business plan, I thought he'd be happy. I was wrong. He accused me of providing Liam a place to play whenever he wanted. When I kindly reminded him that Liam Page does not need me for anything, he scoffed and left the table.

We were partners until I screwed it all up. Now I need to fix it and don't know how. Everyone says you hit a rough patch in life, but this is more like road rash that won't go away and I need it to because I miss Nick and I hate that he's hurting because of me.

When Jenna arrives, the contractor is following behind her, staring at her ass. Some men are so crass. She comes behind the counter and drops her purse in the cabinet before turning her attention on him. She thinks he's a customer and he just might be after today. Maybe I can bribe her into dating him while construction is going on so I can get a good deal.

I've just turned into not only a shitty fiancée but an equally bad friend. I need help.

"Hi, Harry," I say over Jenna.

"Hey, Josie," he replies while looking at Jenna. I snap my fingers to get his attention. It takes forever for his eyes to finally meet mine. Great, now he'll be distracted by Jenna the whole time he's here.

"Let's discuss my plans next door," I say grabbing the keys and walking around the counter. I pull the sleeve of his shirt to follow me and don't let go until we are safely outside. I whack him in the arm. "What the hell, Harry?"

"She's beautiful."

"Yeah, well she's off limits. You're here to work and she doesn't date so don't get any ideas." I open the door to the adjacent building. Harry follows me in. I like his work. He renovated the flower shop for me. I know I can trust him.

"I was thinking of opening the wall here," I point to the adjoining wall. "And making the back wall either coolers or put a larger walk-in right over in that corner. This side of the room," I say walking to the other side, "has backyard access so I'd like to be able to have a greenhouse. And in the corner by the second window I'd like to put a stage for performing. The counter will go right there." I point the opposite wall.

Harry starts making notes and begins measuring the

walls. He knocks on the walls and writes notes where he was knocking. "I can start tomorrow if you're ready?"

"I'm ready," I reply quickly. I'm eager to start and bring a new aspect to my business.

"Will you want a new sign for out front?"

I nod. "Yeah, I think so. I'll order all the equipment and you can take care of the rest?"

"Uh huh," he says while writing on his notepad. "I'm going to have to hire someone for a sound system."

"That's fine, Harry. I trust you." I leave Harry to finish his assessment and head back to the shop. It will be nice once the wall comes down. I know my idea is grand, but I have a vision and I plan to make sure it succeeds.

"Who was that?' Jenna asks as soon as I walk in the door. I can't tell by her expression if she was happy to be gawked at or disgusted.

"That was Harry. He's the contractor working on the expansion. I told him you were off limits."

"Good, thanks. I mean I know I've been here for three years, but I'm just not ready." She bundles the bouquet she's working on and wraps it in purple and gold paper. I love that we allow the customers the option of different colored paper. Most florists only offer green or newsprint. I like to add character to my flowers.

"I brought you something that came in my email this morning," Jenna says motioning to the counter. I pick up the piece of paper, reading the headline and looking at her.

"What's this?"

"When I started here I signed up for these mailing lists about being a florist. I didn't want you to think you could never take a day off, so I needed to learn. Anyway, it came today and I thought it might interest you."

Learning over the counter I read about the convention.

The opportunity to take classes, workshops and attend a trade show all in one convenient location it says. I've never attended one before, but with the expansion maybe it's time I start expanding my knowledge base.

"I should do this."

"Yes you should," she replies. When I look at her, she's grinning from ear to ear.

"What?"

"It's in Los Angeles and its next week."

I look back at the paper, sure enough, it is. My heart pounds just a bit faster at the thought of seeing Liam. What if I saw him walking down the street? Would he hug me if he saw me or ignore me? I'm being silly. It's a huge place. I'll never run into him.

"You should go," she says putting her hand on my arm. "You and Nick need a break. Maybe a few days apart will do you some good."

"Jenna—"

She puts her hand up, stopping me. Her head shakes slightly. "Don't, Josie. I'm not saying go there and cheat on Nick. I'm saying, go and work and if you meet the father of your son for dinner or coffee to discuss the upcoming holidays, then so be it. Just don't deny yourself this opportunity."

Jenna turns her back and finishes up her orders. I stand, my hip against the counter, reading the blurred words over and over again. All I can think about is seeing Liam, but I know that doing so would hurt Nick and I refuse to hurt him anymore than I already have.

I SIT IN THE DARK, still clutching the flyer. Jenna has

long left, the shit-eating grin still plastered on her face when she shut and locked the door behind her. I wanted to ask her why she would give this to me, but could never get the words out.

My thumb hovers over Liam's name. I'm not sure if I should call him. What if he says it's not a good idea or tells me to come but he's busy? Can I take the rejection?

I jump when a horn blares. My thumb inadvertently hits the call button, his and Noah's faces light up my screen. It's a picture I took when neither of them knew I was in the room. My hand shakes as I bring my phone to my ear. I listen through the rings and hope he doesn't answer.

"Hello." He doesn't sound out of breath or rushed when he answers, just calm and very Liam.

"I didn't mean to call," I say barely audible.

"I'm happy you did. I like hearing your voice."

"You shouldn't say things like that to me."

He laughs. "Well, if you expect me to lie or keep my emotions in check, it's not going to happen. So what do I owe the pleasure of your call? I'm very happy to hear your voice."

"God, are you this smooth with all your women?"

"There are no women, Josie. I promise you. So what's up?"

"I'm thinking of coming to L.A. for a trade show and wanted to know if you wanted to get coffee?"

Liam is silent for a moment. I can hear him breathing so I know he didn't hang up on me. "Are you bringing Noah?"

"No, this is next week and he has a Boy Scout camping trip. It would just be me. I mean if you're busy and don't have time, I understand. I know this is short notice and you probably have a bunch of parties and whatever to—"

"Josie!"

"What?"

"Shut up for a minute, geez. I want to see you, Jojo. I'll make the time. Where will you be staying?"

I unfold the flyer and look. I tell him where and he starts to laugh. "What's so funny?"

"Nothing, it's just that I live on the top floor."

I'm going to be spending the weekend in Liam's hotel. I think I'm in trouble.

23

LIAM

Josie is in L.A. today. In fact, she's downstairs in the convention center. I know this shouldn't be the only thing on my mind, but it is. I snagged one of the agendas for the trade show she's attending so I could keep my schedule clear. I've canceled two interviews – which did not go over well with Sam. She demanded, in a very high pitched screech, that I was to tell her who I knocked up while I was gone so she could do damage control. I've told her repeatedly that no one is pregnant, but she's not buying it. Her obsession with pregnancy is starting to scare me.

I wanted to meet Josie at the airport, but didn't dare ask her when her flight was arriving. I need to try and keep my cool even though I'm tempted to visit that side of the hotel and see if I can find her. We're having dinner tonight in my penthouse. I'm not taking her out of this hotel if I can manage it. I don't want her face splattered all over the gossip columns and rag TV shows. I don't even want the press to know her name. They'll start digging and that will put Noah in harm's way.

I shouldn't bring her to my room though. I know it's a mistake, but since I kissed her the night we told Noah about me being his father, I haven't been able to stop thinking about her. I know she's off limits. I know she's marrying another man, but I'm a glutton for punishment because having her in my space is enough for me, even if I can't touch her like I want to.

I look at the nameless cat sitting on the window sill and have to laugh. Noah can't wait to meet him. I've started looking for houses in Beaumont, something for me and Noah. Most of the houses there are good size, but I want a nice big yard and something with a basement that I can soundproof and turn into a studio. As much as I'd love to take a week off a month, deadlines are looming and this new album is coming together rather quickly. That means Sam will schedule another tour and put us back out on the road and farther away from Noah. I should've stalled on these songs.

A knock and announcement of room service puts a smile on my face. The front desk knows to give Josie an access card to my floor when she presents herself there in a few minutes. My nerves are on edge.

Opening the door, it's one of my regular delivery guys. This is good and bad. Good because I know him. Bad because he knows I eat alone and I'm definitely not eating alone tonight.

"Having company tonight Mr. Page?" he asks as he pushes the service cart into my room.

"No, Michael, just a meeting."

"This is some fancy and romantic dinner for a meeting."

"She's writing a book. I need to make sure she gets everything right. I don't want to be misquoted," I lie through my teeth.

"I hear that Mr. Page. Where do you want it?"

I want it in my bedroom, but that's just not an option. Over by the balcony is where we are going to eat, but I don't want room service to know that. I have no doubt Michael is going to gossip when he gets back down downstairs.

"We'll eat at the table," I say. He nods and pushes the cart over there, unloading and setting the table. I look at my watch, counting the seconds as they go by. He seems to be moving extremely slow. She's going to show up any moment.

"I put the extra bottle of champagne in your refrigerator, sir."

"Thank you, Michael." I hand him his tip and he's out the door. I breathe a sigh of relief. Now I just need Josie.

A soft knock sends me running to the door. I look down at what I'm wearing and bang my head against my fist. I should've changed. We're having a nice dinner and I'm showing up in jeans and a t-shirt. I open the door, my breathing stops. Standing before me is my girl. Her hair is up in a bun, a few strands hanging down all around her head. She's wearing a red v-neck dress that is showing me every curve that I remember and some new ones that I think I need to learn. Her dress stops at her knees and is quickly met by black knee-high boots. An image of me on my knees with the zipper in my mouth flashes before my eyes. Definitely something I want to try... with her... someday.

"God, Jojo. You're beautiful."

She blushes and runs her hands down the front of her dress. Moving aside to let her in, I inhale deeply when she passes so I can take in her scent. Pure flowers, very Josie. When she walks by my eyes feast on her backside, I swallow hard.

I slam the door causing her to jump. When she turns

her blush hasn't subsided and I hope it's because I do that to her and not because she's having second thoughts about being up in my room.

"I'm sorry I didn't mean to startle you."

"It's fine. I'm just a little jumpy today."

I understand the nerves. I've had them all day. I guide her into the living room area. Her eyes go wide when she sees the view from the glass wall.

"Wow, Liam this is..." she steps over to the wall, leaving me standing here and giving me the opportunity to watch her take in the bright lights of Los Angeles. She shakes her head, her hand covers her mouth.

"What's wrong?" I ask, keeping my distance.

"I can see why you left me. It's beautiful."

"It's pretty spectacular at night when it's like this, during the day, not so much." I come up behind her and place my hand gently on her hip. "Look over there." I point to where the spotlights are lighting up the sky. "That's a movie premiere. There are probably a couple thousand screaming fans down there right now."

"Have you ever been?" she asks. She closes her eyes and leans her head my shoulder. I have to remind myself to be a good boy.

"I have. It's an experience." I hold her like this for a moment, wishing it could be all night. "Josie, what you said, about me, leaving you for this. It's not like that. I wanted you with me every minute of every day, but I didn't think you'd come."

She doesn't reply and does the unthinkable and turns away from me to look around the room. She touches my Grammys, my gold records and the album covers I have on the wall.

"You've done really well for yourself."

"I was determined. I had a lot to prove."

"To who?"

"Me, mostly." I bring her toward the table, pulling a chair out for her. She sits and I push it in slightly. She pulls her napkin to her lap while I pour glasses of champagne. "Sorry I didn't dress up. This is my usual attire until I'm at one of those events." I motion to the window.

"Do you go often?"

I pull the covers off our food and sit down. "It depends on what I have going on. If I have a new album coming out, yes I go. It's free publicity and I'll be able to push the release date or talk about the single playing on the radio. I've had to go a few times because I, well actually my band, have contributed to a soundtrack."

Josie is quiet for a few minutes. She focuses on her food and I wonder if I said something wrong. I hope that I didn't, but she has to see how different my life is here over what we would've had in Beaumont.

"Can I ask you a question?"

"Of course," she says before taking a sip of her champagne.

"Would you have liked all of this? The lights, noise, the traveling and long hours. Not being able to live a peaceful life. There would be no walking down the street without someone taking your picture. You'd worry about what or who you were wearing to a premiere and people would be your friends because of who you are or married too. Is this something you could see for yourself?"

Josie puts down her fork, bringing her napkin to her lips. When she pulls it away, she smiles at me. "If you're asking me today if I could live like this, the answer is no. I've lived such a quiet life for the last ten years I wouldn't know what to do with all of this if I had to do it now. But had you said you were giving me an option of never seeing you again or moving here so you could try your hand at music, I would've gone with you. I would've left that night because you were my life, Liam."

"I didn't think you would and I didn't want to hear you tell me no or belittle me for wanting something different. I needed to try this."

"And now that you have?"

I shake my head. There is no right answer for this one. It won't matter what I say because I've lost ten years with her and our son. "I love my life, Jojo, and I hate it all in one. I love what I do – making music and entertaining people. I wrote a whole album that you and Noah inspired in two weeks. That feeling alone is indescribable for me." I lean forward and pull her hand into mine. "But not having you in my life has been tough. I miss everything about you and I wake up in the morning and think 'what the fuck did I do' because I had the most beautiful girl on my arm and gave her up for what... this?" I spread my arm out. "I live in a hotel because it's convenient. They do my cooking, cleaning and laundry if I want them to. I have someone who dictates what interviews I can give and whose designer clothes I'm going to wear. I'm her fucking puppet because I pay her to do this job and I think about giving it up, but then I remember why I do it and can't."

"You're really good at what you do."

"Thank you," I say bringing her hand to my lips. I place small kisses along her knuckles. I reluctantly let her hand go and pour us some more champagne.

"Are you trying to get me drunk?"

I give her my patented look. Her mouth drops open, her eyes glaze over. Josie has just met Liam Page.

I've been able to avoid most of Liam's looks until this one. I know my mouth is hanging open like a fish, my tongue dry. I cross my legs to ward off the throbbing between my thighs. I sit back and he smiles, shaking his head. He gets up, stopping behind me.

"What's wrong, Jojo?" he whispers seductively, his nose skimming behind my ear making my breathing labored and unsteady. When he bites my ear, I squirm in my seat. I have to move away from him before I do something I regret.

He starts laughing and plants a kiss on my cheek. When he returns from the kitchen he has another bottle of champagne, and now I'm in trouble.

"That wasn't nice," I say, trying to be stern.

"You know, if you're having a bit of an issue, I could help you." His eyes are devious as he stares at me. He swallows and I watch his adams apple move, remembering the countless kisses I've placed there.

"I've heard about this look that you give women."

"I didn't peg you for one who bought those trashy magazines."

"Jenna does and she told me. She wants to go to one of your concerts, she didn't know who you were until you came to town. I mean she knew, just not the connection.

"Remind me to send her tickets and a backstage pass."

"I don't think so," I reply. I don't think I want any woman to ever experience that look from Liam again.

"Josephine Preston, are you jealous?"

I pick up my glass and down some liquid courage. "She thinks you're hot. I know she's my friend, but I also know she hasn't dated in three years and if you did that she'd turn to a pile of goo and fall down at your feet. I'd hate to think..."

"I only have eyes for one woman, period." Liam sets down his knife and fork, resting his elbows on the table and folding his hands together. "When I saw you, I knew I had made a mistake. I should have never left or at least come back for you. My life is better with you in it, Josie. I'm not going to do anything to jeopardize that."

"I'm getting married," I choke out. Nick and I talked about setting a date when I get back and I've already let Liam touch me and kiss me. My god, what does that make me?

"Where's your ring?"

I look down at my bare left finger. Of all the times Nick has asked, he's never shown me a ring. Maybe he thinks I don't want one, although I'm not sure where he'd get that idea from because I do want one. I want to wear what he's picked out to symbolize his love for me.

"He's an idiot." Liam throws his napkin down on the table. "If you were mine, that finger would not be bare, especially if you were visiting your ex-boyfriend."

"He doesn't know I'm here. I mean he knows I'm in Los Angeles, but he doesn't know I'm here with you."

Liam pushes his chair out and stands. He picks up a remote and music starts. He walks the three steps to me and holds out his hand. "Dance with me."

"I shouldn't," I whisper, unable to look at him.

His fingers trail my jaw. He gently raises my face; my eyes find his. "You want to, Jojo, don't deny it. I won't tell."

I push my chair back and stand, taking his offered hand. He walks us to the middle of the living room, hitting a switch on the wall to dim the lights. We stand in the glow from the city lights.

His hands press gently on my waist, his fingers spread out to feel more of me. I keep my hands on his shoulders, a safe distance from his hair, while our bodies sway to the soulful melody coming from his stereo. He pulls me closer, his hands moving up my back. One hand comes forward, moving strands of hair away from my face.

Every inch of my body is on fire. The look in his eyes tells me he wants me, I just have to make the first move. His hand roams down my back, cupping my ass, pushing me closer into him. I haven't forgotten what it's like to be with him; I don't think I ever will. We taught each other everything. We explored each other's bodies, learning as we became lovers. I knew how to satisfy him, knew every secret spot to make him shiver and squirm.

His other hand trails up my arm, picking up my hand and placing it on the nape of his neck. My fingers push into his hair and he groans. His eyes fluttering closed. He's grown it out since I first saw him in Beaumont. I like it this way best.

His hand grips my hip, pulling me even closer, grinding into me. I bite my lip to keep my mouth from falling open. Anticipation builds. The desire is there and he knows it. He's studying me, marking me as his prey. His eyes are hooded, smoky. He licks his lips, watching me for some hint that he can take the next step.

I can't give it to him.

I won't.

"Who are we listening to?" I ask hoping to break up the tension in the air. The singer's voice is hoarse and sexy. I could listen to it for hours. Liam bends me back a bit, the swell of my chest even with his mouth. He kisses each breast before kissing the valley of my cleavage.

"Me," he says against my skin.

"Who are you singing about?"

He carefully pulls me forward. My hands instantly weave back into his hair. He looks at my mouth then my eyes.

"You."

"Me?"

"Only you, Jojo." He says as his lips meet mine. He has one hand in my hair, the other splayed on my back. He is soft, ever so lightly pulling my bottom lip between his teeth. When he releases, he's back on my mouth, tracing my lower lip with his tongue. I should push him away, but I can't.

I want this.

I want to feel him.

I meet his tongue with mine. He moans, setting a slow and steady pace. Our bodies work themselves into a heated frenzy. His mouth leaves mine, trailing kisses down my jaw to my ear and to my neck. He holds me securely in his hands as he sings to me with words and kisses.

My hand slides under his shirt, the sensation of his skin under my fingertips is intoxicating.

I need to stop this. I have Nick to think about, but this is Liam and I...

He left me.

My hands find his shoulders and push. His arms go lax as he looks at me. He shakes his head and steps away from me. His hands tug at his hair.

"I'm sorry—"

"You don't need to apologize. I shouldn't have done that," I say. My hands feel empty without him. I want to reach for him, hold his hand, but that would send the wrong message. It's bad enough we've gone this far. I'm engaged and this is cheating. "I should go."

He doesn't say anything, just nods. He's staring out into the city lights probably remembering why he left me. I look back at him one last time before opening the door.

"Josie, wait." I pause and turn around, closing the door behind me. He's there, by my side, before I can catch my breath. "I'm sorry. I should have never put you in that position. I was being selfish and only thinking about myself and how much I miss you. You were here, in my home, and I couldn't resist. You're a temptation for me and right now I just want to pick you up and carry you to my bed and not let you leave."

"I can't. I'm—"

Liam puts his finger to my lips. "I'm just telling you what I want so my signals aren't mixed. I want you to know exactly how I feel because the last time I kept secrets, I ruined us."

"We can't do this, Liam. I'm getting married."

"Then I'll wait. Forever, if I have to." He places a lingering kiss on my cheek, holding me to him. "I want to see you tomorrow."

"I don't know."

"I'll be a perfect gentleman. I promise you."

I nod as he opens the door for me. With one last look I

walk out of his place. I look back as I wait for the elevator and he's standing against the door, hands in his pockets, watching me. The ding from the arriving car breaks my heart.

25

___

LIAM

For the first time in years I'll be sitting down for a Thanksgiving dinner. When Katelyn called and extended the invitation I immediately took her up on it. I knew that spending the holiday with Josie and Noah was completely out of the question. After she was here for her trade show, things between us became strained and that, once again, was my fault.

I know I screwed things up with her and probably for her.

Arriving in Beaumont is better this time. I'm staying at Katelyn's house instead of a hotel and for that I'm thankful. I'll be able to spend quality time with Noah in the comfort of a home. He and I will spend Saturday looking for houses because on Friday I promised to watch the twins so Katelyn could go shopping.

I drive through town hoping to catch a glimpse of Josie at her shop. I know it's a long shot, but I'm desperate. I'm in love with a girl that can't love me back. I gotta take what I can get. I drive by twice, both to no avail.

Pulling into the driveway, at Katelyn's house, Peyton

stands and waves from the back of the pick-up truck. When I step out of my rental, she's jumping up and down yelling my name.

"Hey, Miss Peyton." I open the trunk and pull out my luggage. I packed extra clothes this time just in case I decide to stay past a week. Last time I was here for almost two weeks and ended up buying more clothes. I also pick up the Apple bag containing the laptop I purchased for the girls. I want to be able to video call Peyton and watch football with her so she's not alone on Sundays.

"What's in the bag, Uncle Liam?" I stop in my tracks when she calls me uncle. This was something Mason and I joked about many times when we would talk about our lives and the direction we were heading.

"Oh, nothing important just presents for you, Elle and your mom." The excitement on her face is worth bringing gifts. I'm not sure how Katelyn is going to react to them or if she'll even accept them.

Peyton guides me into the house. The smell of pumpkin pie makes my stomach growl. Katelyn's in the kitchen with an apron tied around her waist, as is Elle. Katelyn comes over to meet me. I kiss her on the cheek as she hugs me.

"Thanks for inviting me."

"Well, Peyton needed someone to watch football with tomorrow." I look at Peyton who shrugs. She's holding her sisters hand eagerly waiting for the presents I've brought. "Peyton will show you to your room."

I follow Peyton downstairs. "Remember the TV?"

"Of course," I reply. We turn the corner into Mason's room and I see why she brought it up. There's a gaping hole in the middle of it. "What happened?"

"Elle got mad and threw daddy's football into it."

I don't know what to say so I just shut my mouth. I've

only been a parent little over a month so I'm not qualified to handle these types of things. Peyton opens a door and walks inside.

"This is the doghouse."

I can't help but laugh because not only is this where Mason likely spent a lot of time, but it's decorated as such. I need to thank Katelyn for bringing humor into my life. Peyton leaves me to get settled. I text Noah to let him know that I'm in town and at Katelyn's, and that we'll see each other on Friday. I wanted to see him tonight or tomorrow, but Josie was adamant that he spend the holidays with her, Nick and their families. I couldn't really argue with her, so I accepted what she said and left it alone.

I bring my bag of goodies with me when I come upstairs. Katelyn is sitting at the table, her fingers rubbing her temple. I see an open checkbook and a pile of bills. I pull out the chair and sit down across from her and tap her lightly. She tries to smile, but she's been crying.

"Where are the girls?"

She picks up her papers and pushes them aside. "They're watching a movie in their room."

"Do you want to talk about those?" I point to the pile of bills. She shakes her head, wiping the tears away from her face.

"I can't make it. I have to sell the house."

I know I'm over-stepping my boundaries, but I can't help it. I grab her checkbook and look. There isn't enough to buy a gallon of milk in there. I reach for the pile of bills, but her hand comes down on mine.

"Let me help, Katelyn. I know you don't want handouts, but please listen. I have the means to take care of this. For Mason."

"I can't, Liam."

"You can't sell your house either. This is the home your girls shared with their dad, it has memories." I reach across and pull her hand into mine. "I want to do this for the girls. Please let me fix all of this."

She pulls her hand away to cover her face as she sobs. She nods, giving me her consent to take care of her bills. I plan to do a lot more.

I try to convince Katelyn that she needs a night out, but she refuses and pushes me out the door. I want her to come with me to Ralph's. I told Ralph that I'd do some gigs for him if he charged a cover. I want him to make some profit off me. It's the least I could do.

I get there early, the door propped open by a cinder block. I walk in to see him setting up the stage and go over to give him a hand.

"Hey, you're early."

"Yeah, I wanted to talk to you about something before I went on tonight." I tape down the electrical plugs for the amp and mic, making sure they'll be out of my way.

"What's up?"

"I'd like to do a benefit show for Katelyn Powell and the girls. I'll bring my band in and have my manager set it up. We'll play for free, but all the door fees need to go to Katelyn."

Ralph rubs his chin, his fingers going back and forth. "Absolutely!" he says with much enthusiasm. "Hell, tonight all the door charges will go to them. I'll have the missus make up some signs."

"Thanks, Ralph." I pat him on the back before he leaves the stage. I head back out to my car and get my keyboard and guitar. I told Ralph we'd really do the show up tonight. As soon as my gear is set up I run through a quick sound check. I won't be worrying about mic quality, but I do want to hear how the acoustics are in this place with an amp.

Women mill around the stage, some dressed in the shortest of skirts. Before returning to Beaumont for Mason, I would've taken one of them into the back for a quick fuck, but not now. Not a single one of them appeals to me. In fact, the way they are dressed just shows how easy they are.

As soon as the lights dim, I start my set. I'm doing twelve songs tonight, maybe an encore. I haven't decided yet. I start with Unforgettable. This will be our second single. Sam will kill me if she finds out I played it, but I don't really care.

In between songs I take a few requests from the fans up front. They request some of my earlier hits, but most of the songs I'm playing tonight are off our recent album.

"Okay, I have time for one more request," I say to the crowd.

"I have a request," a male voice yells from the front of the bar. I look for the person to come forward, but no one is moving.

"I have a request, I said!"

"Okay, let's hear it," I reply, still waiting for the man to show himself.

"My first request is that you leave my fucking fiancée alone. My second request is that you leave Beaumont and never come back. And my third request of the night is that you tell your son how much of a fucking loser you are so that when you leave, he won't fucking hate me for driving you out of town."

Drunk people suck.

Nick is finally in view, he's swaying from side to side. He has a friend on each side trying to get him to sit down.

Everyone in the bar is quiet, half looking at me, the other half at him.

I strum my guitar to get the crowd's attention.

"Can't you answer me, Westbury?"

"No, Ashford. This isn't the time or place."

"Let's go outside then hot shot."

I shake my head and remove my guitar. "Sorry guys, show's over. But don't forget about the benefit concert we'll be doing."

I pack up my guitar and keyboard as Ralph apologizes in my ear about Nick. I tell him not to worry about Nick, that he's drunk. I look around the bar for him, but he's gone so I decide to call it a night.

When I step outside he's leaning against a truck. I'm in no mood to talk to him if he's like this. I set my gear in the backseat and turn to face him. He's sauntering over to me, unable to walk a straight line.

"Where are your buddies?"

"I don't need them to kick your ass, Westbury."

"I'm not fighting you," I say as I move away from my car.

"Well, I want to fight you. I need to fight for my family. Ever since you showed up here, it's all Liam this and Liam that. My dad this, my dad that. I'm his fucking dad, not you. I raised him. I cleaned up the skinned knees and taught him how to play football all while you were off screwing half the female population.

"And my soon to be wife... god what a bitch she's been all because of you—"

"Don't call her a bitch, Nick. You're drunk and you're going to regret it." I pull out my phone and text Josie telling her that she needs to come get him before something bad happens.

"You left her. I picked up the pieces. I waited patiently

for her to look in my direction and when she finally did, I was so happy. But no, you had to come back and screw shit up for us. She loves me, not you so why don't you pack your shit and leave. Do us all a favor and get out of here. I want my family back and you're in the way."

"He's my son, Nick. I didn't abandon him. He deserves to know me."

Nick shakes his head and leans against my car, his head hanging. If I didn't know better I'd think he's crying. I get where he's coming from, but there's no way I'll give up Noah. Josie – yeah I'll wait for her, but Noah's mine and I intend to stay for him.

Josie pulls up, the bright lights from the car shining against Nick. He looks up and shields his eyes. I stand, in the same spot I was in when he started in on me, waiting for her to get out of the car.

"Hey baby," he says when he sees Josie. She offers me a small smile before pulling Nick into her arms. "I love you, Josephine. Tell me you love me. Tell Westbury that you choose me over him."

"Come on, Nick, let's go home."

"Tell him, Josie. Tell him so he'll go away and leave us alone. I want my fiancée back."

"He can hear you. I don't need to repeat what you're saying."

"Did you sleep with him in L.A.?"

"No, Nick. Now come on. You're drunk and I want to go home." Josie pulls Nick to her car, helping him inside. She doesn't look at me before she gets in the driver's seat or when she pulls out.

I get in my car and slam the door.

A perfect night ruined.

26

JOSIE

I spent another night on the couch, but this time I didn't sleep. I stared at the floor, my hands, the picture window that Nick installed for me a few years ago – anything to keep my mind off the utter mess my life has become and the passed out man upstairs in my bedroom sleeping off his drunken ass.

When Liam texted me last night, I wanted to cry. Not just for me, but for Nick too. Through everything that has happened, everything that I've done wrong, no one stopped to consider his feelings. I should've put him first. He's the one who has been there from day one, even before we were dating. He was there for Noah.

And now he's suffering because of my inability to see past Liam. I never thought Liam would come back.

But he's here and he makes me feel things I haven't felt since I stopped thinking about him. Maybe I never truly stopped. Maybe I just masked my feelings. I love Nick, but not the same way I love Liam. Liam was my first everything, but that's not enough to give up Nick.

When the coffee is done brewing, I pour Nick a cup

and place it on a tray with some dry toast and bacon. He's rarely like this, so I don't know how he'll handle a hangover, especially when we sit down to dinner with his parents in a few hours.

Climbing the stairs carefully, I push our bedroom door open with my toe. He's lying on his back, arms spread out. Had I been in bed, he would've knocked me in the face. Standing there, I study him, his blonde hair in disarray. The comforter is on the floor at the foot of the bed, a sheet is covering him from the waist down. I watch as his defined chest moves up and down with his breath. I'm just happy he didn't throw-up in the middle of the night.

I set the tray down on the nightstand, walk over to the window and open it for some fresh air. I crawl onto the bed next to him and can't help but reach out and touch him. I run my fingers down his chest, tracing his muscles. He flinches a bit and bats my hand away. I try to stifle a laugh, but I know he can hear me.

Suddenly, his arm wraps around my waist and pulls me across his chest, his other arm resting on my back. He's awake. He holds me as I snuggle in closer.

"How do you feel?"

"Like death." His reply is hoarse. He has to cough a few times to clear out his throat.

"You had a pretty rough night."

He doesn't say anything. He rolls us over so that we're face to face. He bunches up the hem of my shirt like he's going to get lost if he's not holding onto me. "I drank too much and have a feeling I did something stupid."

I nod, not wanting to embarrass him. He's done enough of that himself. I move his hair away from his face, a face that I fell in love with years ago.

"I made you some breakfast."

"Are you going to tell me what I did?"

I shrug. "I don't know it all, just the bit when I got there. I guess you and Liam exchanged some words because he texted me that you were drunk so I came and got you."

Nick closes his eyes and buries his head into my chest. He pulls me closer, needing the same reassurance I do that everything will be okay.

"I'm trying, Josie. I really am. I don't know what happened last night. I walked into Ralph's and everyone was going crazy for him and all I could think about it is how I'm losing everything to this guy who doesn't deserve it. I started drinking and I know I said something to him, but I can't remember."

"I'm not going anywhere, Nick."

After breakfast, Nick showered while Noah and I waited for him to come downstairs. I'm certain Liam won't say anything about their fight, especially in front of Noah, so I told Nick we don't need to talk about it anymore.

He's dressed in dark gray trousers and a white button down, his tie hanging open and loose when he comes down the stairs. I meet him at the bottom step and tie it for him. He pulls me into a deep embrace until Noah starts heckling us.

"You just wait until you get a girlfriend," Nick says as he helps me into my coat.

"No way! Girls have cooties and don't understand football." Nick holds his hand up for a high-five that Noah hits dead on. I roll my eyes. My boys are incorrigible.

Thanksgiving dinner at Nick's parents' house is always interesting. My parents join us and it's a huge feast. Christmas is a much smaller event. As we all gather around the table, holding hands for prayer, I'm thankful that my family is whole – at least for today.

After dinner the guys have cleaning duties while the women pour over the Black Friday ads for tomorrow's shopping excursion. I haven't a clue as what to get Noah and Nick for Christmas and I'm hoping that I'll see something that will spark my interest.

Nick and I are able to dodge marriage talk, even though we've talked about setting a date after the holidays. We want to get through Christmas without the pressure of people asking where we're getting married.

Noah, Nick, and the other men head outside to play some football. The weather's changing and I know it will snow soon. Noah has one more game before his season is done and Liam has promised to be there.

Liam. I don't know what to do about him. Sometimes I wish he hadn't come back or seen Noah that day. I think things would be so much easier, but then Noah wouldn't know his dad. Then I think that every kid should know both their parents given the chance. Elle and Peyton will barely have any memories of Mason when they're older. I don't want that for Noah.

The guys come back in, rosy-cheeked and dirty. Nick pulls me into a kiss, slipping his freezing hands underneath my sweater. I push him away, but he holds me tight. "I love you," he says against my lips.

"I love you, too."

He pushes my hair behind my ear. "I want to head over to Katelyn's."

"Why?" I ask. Liam's there and I don't want them fighting, especially in front of Noah.

"I need to apologize to Liam. I don't want last night hanging over our heads and I think Noah would like to see him. Maybe we can stop at home and he can pack a bag and stay with Liam tonight. Give us some alone time."

"I'd like that," I say before placing my lips to his.

Noah is more than excited to be staying with Liam tonight. When we pull into Katelyn's driveway, Noah is out of the car before Nick has it in park. Nick and I walk hand in hand into Katelyn's house. Noah is already sitting with Liam, trying to push Peyton out of the way. Katelyn is in the chair with Elle. For a brief moment I look at Liam, so comfortable in Katelyn's house and wonder if there could be something between them.

She's been the one to make him feel welcomed, opening her house to him, inviting him to Thanksgiving and now he's lying on the floor, Peyton resting on his stomach, like he owns the place.

He sits up when he sees me staring at him, Nick behind me. I know I'm imagining things, but can't help it. My mind is going crazy here with images of them together. Katelyn closes her book and moves a sleeping Elle so she can sit up and greet us.

"What's going on?" she says, yawning.

"We thought Liam would like to see Noah," I say, eyeing Liam. "But if you guys are busy..."

"I don't think watching TV constitutes being busy, Josie. I'm glad Noah's here," Liam says to me. The way he looks at me tells me he knows what I'm thinking. We've been down the jealousy road before and it's just reared it's very ugly head with me again.

"Make yourselves at home. I'll put on a pot of coffee." Liam gets up and helps Katelyn with Elle. My eyes follow him down the hall as he takes her to her bed. Apparently he puts the girls to bed now too.

"Westbury," Nick says when Liam walks back into the room. "Let's go outside and talk." Liam doesn't say anything he just nods and walks out the side door leading to the driveway. Nick kisses me on the cheek and promises to be good.

"I know you want to listen," Katelyn says when she hands me a cup of coffee. She motions for me to follow her into the kitchen.

"Where are they going?" Noah asks before I leave the room.

"Just to talk." I turn back to Katelyn.

"What's going on with you?" she asks sipping on her cup.

"Nothing, just taken aback by how natural everything looked when I walked in, that's all. I guess I didn't expect you to move on so quickly."

Katelyn sprays hot coffee out of her mouth, ruining her white shirt. "Are you kidding me here, Josie? You think Liam and I are... oh god I can't even. I just buried my husband. I have no intention of pursuing anything with anyone. Liam is here because I didn't want him to be alone and I didn't want to be alone on Thanksgiving and Peyton wanted someone to watch football with."

"I just thought—"

"You thought wrong. He only agreed because it gave Noah a place to come and stay until he can buy a house." Katelyn moves to the sink to clean herself up. "In case you didn't know, that man is still head over heels for you."

"I know he is," I mumble. I'm so stupid to think Katelyn would start something with him.

Katelyn wipes her hands on the towel and leans against the counter. "What the hell are you doing, Josie?"

I stare at Katelyn and back at the door before looking at her again. Tears pool in my eyes. I hide my face and fall into her arms.

I f I ever mention buying a house again, someone please shoot me. Noah and I spent all of Saturday and Sunday wandering Beaumont with my excessively hyper real estate agent. The only thing I learned was how to eye roll like a nine year old.

Sarah, Sadie or maybe it was Suzie – I don't remember – showed us house after house, none of which met my requirements. Yes, I may be one person with a kid that I will have occasionally, but that doesn't mean I want a small house. I want two stories with a full basement and attached two-car garage with at least a half-acre of land. I didn't think these requirements were too over-the-top, but apparently they were.

Now Noah and I sit outside this two-story house in the same neighborhood as my parents. I realized that this was exactly what I was looking for, so we drove through looking for a FOR SALE sign. We found one.

We're waiting for the agent to arrive so we can see the inside, but I know I already want it. I can imagine Noah climbing the giant oak trees that surround the property and can see him throwing the football around with his friends in the yard.

This new agent steps out of his car and waves at us. He's short and pudgy with white hair. He looks like a marshmallow.

"Hi, I'm Liam Westbury and this is my son, Noah."

"Nice to meet you, I'm Stu. Let's go in shall we."

We follow Stu up the brick steps. The porch is wide with white pillars in desperate need of a paint job. Stu opens the door allowing Noah and I to step in. Before us is the staircase, open on both sides so you can see into the dining room and living room. The living room has two large windows, one in front and one in back, two more on the side. The kitchen is new, with a nook and all new appliances, and windows facing the back yard. There is a nice sized bathroom just off the kitchen. The dining room faces the front yard with one large window and two that face the side yard.

We head upstairs to the four bedrooms. The master is large with a walk-in closet that leads to a bathroom with shower and Jacuzzi tub. One room is decorated as a nursery which I'd have to change. The other two rooms are the same size. All the rooms have ample natural light. There is one shared bathroom upstairs.

Stu is sitting at the table when we come down. "We're just going to check out the basement," I say as we pass him. He smiles and nods at us and goes back to his paperwork.

The basement is accessed through the kitchen. We stomp down the steps, testing their sturdiness. There is a laundry room and a very large space.

"What do you think, Dad? I'm thinking a man cave like Uncle Mason's over there and your studio there," he points to the wall on the left side of the room.

"Yeah? You know the studio is pretty big. I need a place to set up equipment."

"I think it will be big enough. What do you think?"

I look at my son. He's beaming with excitement. "I like it. Do you think you'll like living here?"

"Yeah, I do."

I put my arm around him and pull him into a half hug. "Let's go buy us a house."

We climb back up the stairs. Stu raises his head when we enter. "We'll take it," Noah blurts out before I have a chance to say anything.

"Yeah, we'll take it."

Stu starts talking about financing and banks. I tell him this will be a cash sale and that I want to move in right away. He calls the homeowners and tells them the deal that is on the table. They accept right away and I agree to show up tomorrow to sign papers in his office.

Noah and I walk around the yard after Stu leaves. He climbs one of the trees and we race across the yard to see who's faster. I may have let him win, but I'll never admit it. We leave the house when the sun starts to set and head to dinner.

Family dining at Deb's is a Beaumont pastime unless you're a Westbury. The first time I went there, I had just gotten my driver's license. When my mom heard about it the next day she was horrified. We Westburys do not degrade ourselves with a place like Deb's.

Whatever.

I love Deb's. Noah and I grab a booth and order our celebratory dinner. He asks when I'll be able to move some stuff in and I tell him that we'll order furniture this week and everything else we'll need. I still haven't been able to come to a decision about leaving L.A. so until then I'll be here for a week or so every month.

We're half way through dinner and Noah drops a bomb. "Mom and Nick fight a lot."

I set my napkin down, placing my arms on the table. "What do you mean? Does Nick hit her?"

"No, at least I've never seen him do anything like that, but I hear them at night arguing. He doesn't think I should be able to spend more than a weekend with you at a time and he doesn't want you buying a house here."

I bring my hands up, resting my chin on them. Noah should not hear them argue about me. It's not fair.

"Listen, buddy. This is a difficult situation for all of us and honestly really unexpected. You know when I came here for Mason's funeral I never expected to find you. I was shocked, hurt and even angry. I didn't know about you and to hear this boy tell me that he saw me kissing his mom on a DVD, I didn't know what to think. So imagine what your mom thought when I showed up or when Nick heard you call me dad. There are a lot of high emotions right now and we're all trying to find the best way to deal with them.

"But don't think that the three of us don't love you. We do, very much. You're our number one priority. Just be patient with your mom and Nick. They'll work out and things will be fine." I'm not sure where all of that came from but I feel good saying it to Noah. He needs to understand that I'm the catalyst for these emotions between Nick and Josie. What I don't understand is Nick. On Thanksgiving he promised to try and be cordial for Noah and Josie's sake. I didn't promise him anything.

I drop Noah off at home and tell him I'll see him tomorrow after school. Right now the agreement is I'll pick

Noah up from school, keep him for dinner and drop him off an hour before bedtime unless he has practice.

I drive by my soon-to-be new house and park out front. I want to see Josie running outside with me and Noah. I want her flowers decorating the front and inside. I want her living here with us as a family.

IT'S Noah's last game of the season. I'm standing in my usual spot with Peyton beside me. She watches Noah like a hawk and I haven't figured out if it's a crush or if she wants to play football. Katelyn says no football, but maybe in a few years she'll change her mind.

Noah is struggling today. He's thrown two interceptions and has fumbled the ball. I'm counting the seconds to halftime so I can ask him what's going on. When the buzzer sounds, I walk over to the sideline to greet him. He takes off his helmet. His unhappy expression makes my heart ache for him.

"What's going on?"

"I don't know. Nothing feels right. I'm seeing everything slow."

"Do you not trust your receivers?"

"Noah, get over here," Nick yells. I know he's the coach, but it's not like I don't know what I'm talking about.

"Trust your receivers, Noah. Throw the pass as it's designed. They'll be there to catch it."

"Thanks, Dad. Sorry you can't come tonight." I look at Noah questioningly. He's with his team before I can ask what he's talking about.

Noah's second half fairs better than the first, but they still end up losing. Noah looks sad and probably angry with himself. He throws his helmet, which I don't approve of at all. I head over to the bench to speak to him about sportsmanship.

"Pick it up, Noah." Nick demands. Noah is standing there, his arms crossed over his chest. "I don't know what you're trying to pull, but it won't fly. Pick it up."

"Noah, what's going on?" I ask, stepping forward and standing next to Nick. Nick takes a deep breath, turns and glares at me.

"This isn't your concern, Westbury. In fact, you're the problem."

"Excuse me?"

"You heard me," he growls.

I look in the stands for Josie. She's standing there, her face frozen as she takes in this scene. There is definitely something going on there that I'm not privy too.

"Get your stuff, Noah. We're going to be late." Noah stares at Nick, not moving. He looks at me with tears in his eyes. I walk over to him and pull him aside.

"Noah, what's the deal?" I ask, bending down to his level.

"There's a team party and Nick said you can't come." I look over my shoulder at Nick who's in a heated conversation with Josie. He makes shit difficult when it could be so easy.

"It's all right, buddy. We can hang out tomorrow."

"No, I want you there and since it's for kids, I should get to pick." My son, the logical one, who knew?

"Tell you what. You go to the party and call me when you're done then I'll come get you and you can spend the night, okay?"

"Mom will say no."

"Leave your mom to me," I say. He leans forward and

gives me a hug. "By the way, if I ever see you throw your helmet again, you'll be sorry. Am I clear?"

"Yes, sir."

"Go pick it up."

I wait a moment before interrupting Josie and Nick. I hate what I'm about to do, but Nick is giving me no other option.

"So, Noah is going to call me when your party thing is over and I'm going to pick him up and take him back to Katelyn's to spend the night."

Nick starts chuckling. "Says who? You?"

"Nick—"

"No, Josie. Set some god damn boundaries with him. You let him walk all over you and Noah played like shit tonight because he's pissed off at me."

"Hey, don't blame Noah. It's not his fault."

"Stay out of this, Westbury."

"You know, Nick, I thought we were cool, but I guess not. Either way, you don't matter in this equation." I hate saying these things because I promised myself I'd treat Nick like a parent. I look at Josie; she looks embarrassed. She should be. "I'll pick Noah up when he calls. If this doesn't work for you, tell me now so I can have my lawyer fax you a custody agreement."

I leave her with the words I never wanted to say, but she's giving me no choice here. I've met every demand of hers and she allows Nick to fight me on spending time with my boy.

No more.

JOSIE

I don't know what I did to deserve the nasty turn my life has taken, but I'd like to know so I can rectify the cluster that has become my life.

The team party is, to put it mildly, an epic disaster. Noah isn't talking to Nick. Nick isn't talking to me. Parents are talking about me. They don't even have the common courtesy to do it behind my back. I can see them pointing and whispering. The head shaking and side glances. They make it seem like I've done something wrong. This incident would be no different if Liam and I were divorced and sharing custody.

I bet I'm being branded the town harlot. So what? I got knocked up by my very steady boyfriend the summer before we left for college and, yes, he left me, but he didn't know about the baby or he wouldn't have. Liam loved me then, unconditionally.

He would've stayed.

And been utterly miserable because he didn't want to play football and that is what I reminded him of, the dream that wasn't his but mine. We would've married and divorced a few years later because I would've held him back from his destiny.

Destiny is such bullshit.

I can't wait to get out of here. I'm done with this football team for the year. I'm done with the pointing, staring and the questions, whether or not Liam will fund the team next year so they can have new uniforms.

My frustration level is reaching an all-time high. I think I need a vacation. Someplace tropical and warm with white sandy beaches and water so blue you look like you're floating in a crystal clear sky. I can close my eyes and feel the warmth on my skin, the sand between my toes and the ocean, its waves calming me with a sweet lullaby.

A place like that calls for romance, a lover's getaway. I can see myself and Nick spending the day sharing a hammock, reading together while he sways us back and forth, gently. I'll snuggle up to him and even though it's hotter than blazes out there, he'll keep me cool. I'll pepper him with kisses and he'll look into my eyes, tell me that he loves me.

Only it's not Nick I see when I look into the eyes staring back at me.

It's Liam.

Noah comes up to me and hugs me from behind. I love my boy. He's the best thing that has ever happened to me. I thank my lucky stars every day that I made the right decision to keep him.

"My dad is outside," he says quietly in my ear. I nod and sit forward, releasing his hold on me. I leave the table. Nick shakes his head while Noah and I walk hand in hand to the front door. Sure enough, leaning up against his car is Liam, his ankles crossed, hands pushed into his pockets.

He doesn't look at me, but smiles at Noah like he hasn't seen him in a week. He loves Noah without question.

"We didn't stop and get him clothes. I'll bring some over."

"No need. I went shopping. He'll have enough at Katelyn's."

It kills me when he talks about Katelyn's. He makes it sound like it's his home. Noah gets in the car and waves to me. Not a kiss goodbye or anything. He knows Nick and I aren't getting along and he wants to be far away from me. I can't blame him.

Liam shuts the door and walks over to me. I'm not prepared to look at him. His expression is indifferent, as if Liam Page is looking at me right now, like I'm one of his conquests who he accidentally fathered a child with.

"You can't take him away from me, Liam. He's all I have."

Liam's eyes are sharp when he looks at me. "I'm not going to take him away from you, Josie, but I'm not going to stand by while Nick acts like this. I tried. I've done everything you've asked of me. I call him daily, I came back. Hell, I bought a fucking house just so he has a place he can feel comfortable in. I'm done bending to appease your boyfriend. I know Nick has raised him, but he's our son, Jojo."

"I know," I choke out.

"I don't know. It feels like Nick is trying to prove a point, like he won you or something. I know he wanted you in high school and it's no secret he and I weren't friends, but this... something's up with him and I don't like it."

Liam leans in and kisses me on the cheek. He leaves without saying goodbye. I watch as his car, the car carrying my whole life, drives away. I turn and look into the window of the pizza parlor. Everyone's laughing and having fun. I lean against the wall and slide down, resting my head in my hands.

"Here, Nick Ashford asked me to give this to you." Katelyn holds up a folded note, waving it back and forth. "Are you and Liam fighting?"

"No, why would you ask that?" I ask while setting my books in my locker.

"I don't know. Why else would Nick Ashford write you a love letter?"

I stand up and look at her. She's smirking, her eye brow raised. "I have no idea." I reach for the note. She moves it fast, keeping it out of my reach.

"What's this?" Mason grabs it out of her hand. Katelyn has an 'oh shit' look on her face when Mason opens it up. He stands still, his jaw clenching. He turns and looks at me. I slink back against my locker.

"Do you have a hard-on for Nick Ashford?"

"No, not at all," I reply, defending myself.

"Wait until Liam sees this," Mason says.

"Sees, what?" Liam bends down to kiss me before turning to Mason. "What's this?" he asks when Mason hands him the piece of paper. Liam looks from the paper to me and back again. "What's this, Josie?"

"I don't know. Katelyn brought it to me. I don't even know what it says."

Liam looks at Katelyn who shrugs. "He gave it to me in history class."

"It says," Liam starts. "Dear Josephine, Do you realize how beautiful you are? I see you in the halls and wish I had the courage to talk to you, but I don't. I wouldn't know what to say. I would like to get to know you better. Call me. Yours, Nicholas Ashford."

Mason and Liam start laughing and it pisses me off. I walk away from them knowing that Nick just bought himself an ass beating. Katelyn should've just handed me the note instead of waving it around.

Before I can turn into my class, a strong hand pushes me through the double doors leading outside. I know its Liam even though he's behind me. He directs me to the football field, his favorite place to hold a conversation, except we aren't talking.

He pushes me up against the concrete wall, my legs wrapping around his hips instantly. His mouth attacks mine, our hands everywhere. "Do you want to call Ashford?" he asks as he moves from my mouth down my neck.

I shake my head and it's the truth. I have no desire to know or talk to Nick Ashford other than being his classmate.

"He's jealous of me, baby. He wants everything I have. Please don't give it to him."

"I won't, I promise."

I press my fingers into my temples, willing away the pressure as the door opens. Nick stands there looking at me. Something has to change. He holds out his hand to help me up, our fingers twisting together as we walk to the car. He seems so much more relaxed when Noah isn't around and I don't like that. I want my son around all the time.

When we get into the house he pushes me up against the wall and kisses me, his tongue eager and rough, as it tangles with mine. He sheds his shirt, pulling at mine. I push him away, but he thinks it's only to gain the space I need to take off my shirt.

"We need to talk," I say without making eye contact.

He lets go of me and leads us into the living room. We both sit. I turn and face him, bringing my knee up underneath me.

"You can't fight with Liam anymore. It's not fair to Noah. I know I screwed things up when I made the decision to tell Noah about Liam, but what's done is done. I can't change it. We have to accept that Liam is part of our lives now and just move forward."

Nick brings my hand to his lips and kisses it. "You're right. I've been an ass and you're also right about moving forward; that's why we're moving."

I look at Nick, dumbfounded. I know my ears must be deceiving me. He has a steady practice here and I'm in the process of expanding my shop. There's no way in hell I'm moving.

"Excuse me, what did you say?" My voice catches in my throat. I can barely breathe.

"I'm taking a sabbatical and we're going to Africa for a year for Doctors Without Borders." I can tell by the look on his face that he's serious and he thinks we're going with him. He made this monumental decision without even consulting me. My choice in telling Noah about Liam is peanuts compared to this.

"No," I whisper. I shake my head. I'm not going anywhere.

"It will be good for us. Noah will learn a lot."

I rip my hand out of his and stand. "Noah and I aren't going, Nick. You don't get to make a decision like this for us without talking to me first. Liam—"

"I don't give a shit about Liam, Josie. Get that through your head. I'm taking my family and we're going."

"No, we're not. You can go, but we're staying here."

Nick stands, moving in front of me. "What are you saying?"

I look at the man I've loved for the past six years. "If you want to go, Nick, then go, but Noah and I are staying here.

Noah has school and his activities and I'm not going to take him away from Liam while they're building a relationship. And I have my shop. I can't just leave, I won't. This... it's not open for discussion."

"So that's it. You're picking Westbury over me?"

I shake my head. "No, Nick, I'm picking Noah."

Noah and I unpack the last box of clothes that I brought from L.A. I've decided to make Beaumont my hometown and will travel back and forth between here and Los Angeles. Harrison and Quinn will join us for Christmas. Harrison doesn't have much family and when I told him about Beaumont, he asked if they could come.

The one thing I haven't done is tell Sam that I've left. I have my penthouse until the end of March at which time I'll have to find temporary digs. I hope Jimmy and Harrison won't mind recording music here.

When I told Harrison about Noah, he was excited and completely on board with my new plan. He said he understood why I needed to make the change and said he'd probably do the same thing if he had just found out about Quinn.

Things with Josie are better but nonexistent and I'm okay with that. She needs time to heal from her break-up and I need time to be a dad. I have a lot of years to make up for.

We're getting a Christmas tree tomorrow. With everything unpacked and put away, the delivery couldn't come at a better time. Katelyn and the girls are coming over to decorate – apparently this is Elle's specialty. Who am I to deny three beautiful women the opportunity to do all the hard work?

The doorbell rings and Noah yells, "I'll get it!" from the top of the stairs. I cringe when I hear him stomping down the stairs. Both Josie and I are afraid he's going to slip and break something, but he isn't listening to either of us. Maybe he'll listen when he's in the emergency room.

I hear a crash and something shattering. I run from the kitchen through the dining room, panic setting in because I can't hear Noah; he's too quiet.

"Noah, are you—"

I stop dead in my tracks. She stands there with casserole spread all over her feet, her hand covering her gaping mouth, eyes watering. I set my hand on Noah's shoulder and look at her. She's aged, but obviously had some work done. I can't tell if she still wears the same red lipstick she did when I was growing up, but I somehow think she hasn't changed much.

"Noah, why don't you go grab some gloves, a towel and a plastic bag and we'll get that cleaned up."

"Okay, Dad."

Noah runs off toward the kitchen. I wait a few beats before looking her in the eyes. She's watching Noah.

"What are you doing here?"

She looks at me, the same cold stare I grew up with. If I didn't know better I'd think she hated me. That maybe I ruined her life.

"I was... he's... casserole and... you're..."

"Are you really speechless or has the vodka finally impaired your ability to function like a normal human?"

"I haven't had a drink in five years," she says.

"Congratulations. You should go before my son comes back. I don't want to explain why we're talking as if we know each other."

"Liam—"

"Don't," I say as I step over the mess she's created on my porch. I shut the door quietly behind me so I can be frank with her. "You don't get to 'Liam' me. You stood by and watched as he threw me out of the house. You're supposed to protect me and you should've been protecting Noah. You live in the same god damn town and he looks just like me, so don't tell me you haven't seen him or Josie around. You should've told me. You were the only one who knew how to get a hold of me and you didn't."

"I'm sorry, I tried, but you know your father. He was adamant."

"I don't want excuses. I missed ten years with him. Ten!"

"Can I meet him?"

I have to look away because looking at her – mascara running down her face like a Sunset Strip street walker – isn't doing much good for me. I hate seeing her like this and, sadly, it's my most vivid memory of her.

"Why should I let you?"

"You shouldn't. I'm not a good person, Liam. I know that. I try, though, all the time to do something good for someone. I'm trying to be independent and not so—"

"Robotic?"

"Is that how you saw me?"

"Yeah it is," I say moving toward the door. "You can

meet him, but Sterling can't. I don't want him anywhere near my son."

She nods and follows me into the house. Noah is sitting on the steps with the supplies in his hands. "What are you doing sitting there?" I ask him.

"You were having a private conversation. I didn't want to interrupt."

"He's so polite." I nod because he is. Josie has raised him well.

"The bathroom is down the hall, Noah and I will clean up this mess."

Bianca Westbury walks down the hall in a home that I own. I swear I never thought I'd see this day in my lifetime. We clean up the mess and Noah hoses down the porch. I'm afraid the steps will ice over tonight, so we'll have to watch that in the morning.

"Who's the lady?' he asks. I want to say a stranger, but she's here and asking for an opportunity that I'm certain Josie wouldn't want her to have. I suppose if she wants to see Noah, she can come over here and do it.

I look over my shoulder to see Bianca standing there wringing her hands. She's cleaned up the best she can, but she's nervous. I've never seen her so unsure of herself. I motion for her to sit down in the living room. She takes one of the wing back chairs while Noah and I sit on the couch.

"Remember when you asked if you could meet my parents?" Noah nods. His eyes light up at the mention of my parents. I wish they didn't, they really aren't anything to write home about. "Noah, this is Bianca Westbury, my mom."

Noah looks at my mom as if he's studying her, learning everything he can about her. She pats down her hair and smiles softly at him. She clasps her hands and then straightens out her skirt again.

Noah looks back and forth between us and shrugs his shoulders. "What do I call you?"

Bianca sits forward, her hands resting on her knees. "Oh, um... I don't know... I... Let's see..."

"I call my nana and papa, nana and... oh that's funny huh, Dad?"

"Dad," Bianca whispers. She looks at me and smiles. "I think if you called me Grandma Bianca that would be okay." She nods and her face lights up. "Yes, I think I'd like Grandma Bianca."

"Okay, that's cool."

"Yes, cool," she says. I start laughing and so does Noah. I don't think Bianca has ever said the word 'cool' before in her life.

"Noah, tell me all about yourself." With those words I'm effectively cut out of this conversation. She moves over to the couch and sits next him. I remember her like this when I was little before things started changing at my house.

I leave them in the living room to get to know each other. I take out my phone and call Josie. She needs to know about my mom coming over and meeting Noah and I'd rather tell her before Noah lets it slip.

"Hi," Josie says on the third ring. We've started talking every day, but I've avoided telling her how I feel. I want her to come to me when she's ready. I'm not into being some-one's rebound and if she wants me it has to be forever. Right now I'm happy having her in my life without drama.

"You wouldn't believe who knocked on the door a half hour ago."

"The delivery man?" She's been giving me so much

crap about the amount of deliveries, but I've never had my own furniture before. I may have gone a bit overboard with a few of my purchases, but I plan to own this house forever and it needs to be furnished properly.

I laugh at her. "Bianca."

Josie only knows how I felt about my parents in high school. I haven't told her about the ultimatum Sterling issued when I decided to leave school. I wait for Josie to say something. There's nothing but silence on her end.

"What is it, Jojo?"

"Did she just show up?"

"She was bringing a casserole to the new people. What's going on?" Her tone is making me curious. She's usually bubbly when we're talking and right now she seems down.

"Nothing," she says, clearing her throat. "So you don't want me to bring dinner tonight?"

Even if the casserole was sitting in my kitchen, I'd still want her to bring dinner because having her in my house, knowing she's not going home to anyone, is a great feeling. I can't wait to carry her up the stairs and lay her down in our bed and keep her there forever.

"I'm expecting you for dinner so you might want to hurry up." She starts laughing and accuses me of using her for her mad food skills, even if she's ordering pizza. I don't deny it, but it's a fine excuse to get her in the door night after night. "I'll see you soon," I say before hanging up.

I peek back into the living room. They're still sitting together deep in conversation. I watch them interacting and wonder how she could've allowed Sterling to be the way he was. She radiates with excitement when she's talking to Noah; why couldn't she have been like this with me?

Nick has been gone for three weeks. The night he told me he was moving, he left. I don't know where he went. Needing a distraction I went to work the next day, giving Jenna a Saturday to do whatever. When I came home his stuff was gone. He didn't have much, just clothes mostly, but I felt his absence when I walked into my bathroom and his shaving cream and toothbrush were missing.

I miss Nick. I miss his laughter, his comfort and how I felt when he held me at night. My heart is not broken. I haven't sat and cried except for the night he left. How I feel is not fair to him. He did the right thing by leaving. He saved us this way. I just want to know if he's okay.

Noah and I are spending Christmas at Liam's with Katelyn and the girls. We'll be one extended family dealing with the loss of a friend, husband and father – together. Katelyn and the girls are with Noah and Liam now, decorating. Liam wanted to wait until I arrived, but I told them to go ahead. I'll have plenty to do later.

In hindsight, Jenna should be working. We're busy. Not

that I'm complaining about having customers, but an additional set of hands would be nice right about now. My delivery boy is definitely adding to his Christmas fund with tips.

"Merry Christmas, Mrs. Potter."

"Oh, Merry Christmas, Josie, I just love your little shop during the holidays. You do such an amazing job with your decorations and flowers.

"Thank you. What can I make for you today?"

"I'm hoping for an arrangement of red roses and white calla lilies to add a little contrast in my entry way."

"Sure thing, Mrs. Potter."

I leave Mrs. Potter while she examines the poinsettias. I direct another customer to the flowers he's looking for before walking to my walk-in cooler. I pick-up the roses and lilies, along with a few other festive flowers before heading back. There's a tall blonde lingering at the register, she doesn't have anything in her hand so I smile at her and tell her I'll be with her in just one moment.

"Hi, excuse me, are you Josephine Preston?"

"I am," I say as I start to arrange the flowers in a crystal vase for Mrs. Potter. She's one of my regulars, always having fresh flowers in her house for something. The new customer just stands there not speaking so I continue to work. I finish up Mrs. Potter's arrangement and take it to the register where she's added other plants. After I ring her up and she pays, I help her carry her purchases to her car.

"Thank you, dear."

"You're welcome. Thank you for shopping here, it means the world to me." She kisses me on the cheek before getting in her car. I hurry back inside; it's freezing out. My hands rub warmth into my arms.

I ring up the remaining customers and start working on

my next order, taking stock of the few customers left in the store.

The blonde walks up to the counter and sets her bag down. Her sunglasses hold her hair back and I look quickly outside for any hint that the sun has come out and see none. Tourists always mark themselves so well. "Can I help you?" I ask.

"I thought we could talk," she says. I have to look at her again to make sure I don't know her from anywhere. I don't.

"Did you want to make an appointment for a bridal consult or is it for something else?"

She smiles when I mention bridal, she must be in love. "Somehow I don't think my man would appreciate it if I made wedding plans without him."

"You'd be surprised. Most don't care."

We laugh. She'll learn that guys just nod and say 'okay, whatever you want honey'. I pull out my appointment book and look at my next available open time.

"We don't really need to meet. I just wanted to give you this," she hands me an envelope – it's manila and fairly light. I look at the return address. It's some lawyer in Los Angeles. This must be the paper work for Noah to become Liam's beneficiary.

"Thanks," I say, setting it aside.

"Aren't you at least interested in what I just handed you?" She leans on the counter, her long red nails catching my attention. Her twisted smile is devious, as if she's planning something harsh and I'm the tail end of the joke.

I pick up the envelope and pull the flap open. Taking out the papers and reading them carefully, anger boils under my skin. He's done what he promised he wouldn't. I put the papers back in the envelope and slide it under the counter next to my purse.

"You really should've just mailed them. It seems like a wasted trip." I try to busy my hands when all I want to do is kick every one out and race to Liam's to pick up my son.

"It's my job to make sure my client's needs are met to the fullest."

"Lucky client," I reply secretly hoping she'll leave. She's done her job. No need to hang around any longer.

"By the way, I'm Sam Moreno," she sticks out her hand. I don't move to shake it. I have no desire to be friendly with her. She pulls her hand back. "Anyway, I'm Liam's manager. From here on out, you'll go through me where your son and Liam are concerned. Also, the last page of the filing I just gave you is for a paternity test."

"A what?" I squeak out.

"Well, you can't expect someone like Liam Page to just hand over cash for a child that might not be his, do you? I mean I'm sure that's what you thought he was going to do when you dumped your kid on his doorstep like a money-grabbing little whore. You may have a desire to milk my client's cash cow repeatedly but I can assure you, I won't let that happen."

"You should go now." I bite my tongue from lashing out. I know she's just doing the job that Liam hired her for, but I want to gouge her eyes out with my shears and watch them bleed down her smug face.

She smiles, picks up her bag and walks out the door.

Customers still linger, but none seem aware of what just took place. I walk up to them calmly and tell them that there has been an emergency and I need to close early. I offer them a discount on their next purchase and promise I'll be open tomorrow. Thankfully they aren't too upset.

The drive to Liam's is messy. I don't even know when it started snowing, but the lightly snow-covered roads make driving difficult. I take in a few deep, calming breaths when I pull into his driveway. He's decorated the outside of his house with white lights. There are candle lights in each window, something I suggested. There's a green wreath with a large red bow hanging on the front door.

For the first time I notice that my name appears on the Santa decoration sitting on the porch. It says *Liam, Josie* and *Noah* live here. I trace our names before knocking.

The door swings open. Liam is standing in front of me. He's confused, his brows push forward. "Why are you knocking?"

I should've practiced what I was going to say. I can't look at him. I just want my son.

"I came to get Noah."

"What do you mean you came to get him? We have plans tonight."

"I... things change. I need to take my son home now."

Liam steps forward, down onto the porch. He closes the door behind him. He's standing on the brick porch barefoot in a t-shirt and jeans. He must be freezing.

"What's going on?" he asks. I step away creating space between us, only for him to step closer. My head shakes, I can't look at him. I won't.

"Jojo," he says as he reaches for me. I bat his hand away.

"Don't call me that."

"What the hell is wrong?" His eyes flash with rage.

"Nothing," I answer sharply. "I want my son and I want to go home."

"Our son," he seethes.

I laugh at his term *our*. "Are you sure about that, Liam Page?"

The look he gives me is one of confusion and hurt. I can

see the pain in his eyes when I call him by his stage name. "What the fuck are you talking about, Josie."

I can't take it anymore. I can't stand here while he plays stupid. I pull the envelope from my purse. "This," I say through tears as I slam it into his chest. "You did this after you promised me you wouldn't. I trusted you... again and you've broken my heart."

Liam pulls the envelope from my hands and tears it open. He reads the first page, then each one after. His face turns white.

When he looks up at me, I see fear.

Josie has only knocked once since I moved in, so when I open the door and she's standing there I know something is wrong. I can tell she's upset. Her stance on my porch is defiant. She's pissed off and I don't know what I did, but I know her anger is because of me.

Stepping out onto the porch is probably the dumbest thing I've done all week. It's cold, snowing and I'm not wearing any socks or shoes. I could care less about not having a jacket on. I'm trying to be serious with her when all I want to do is run back into the warmth of my home.

There is nothing more frustrating than a woman who doesn't tell you what's wrong when you ask her. I want to grab her and shake the answer out of her. She stands in front of me, her shoulders hunched, refusing to look at me, to show me her beautiful eyes that I can read like an open book.

I tear open the manila envelope that she slams against my chest. My eyes read over words like custody, visitation, child support, and California resident. The last page does me in – it says I'm requesting a paternity test to determine if the child known as Noah Michael Preston is my son.

Josie crosses her arms over her mid-section like she's been punched repeatedly. She doesn't bother to wipe the tears that have started cascading down her beautiful face, now marred by deception with my name attached. No wonder she wants to take Noah away. I told her I'd never take him from her and these papers are telling her I am.

This is not what I want. I want us to be a family. I never even thought about this when I found out about Noah. Never in a million years did this thought ever enter my mind.

"Where did you get this?" I demand. I grip the papers, crinkling them in my hand as I shake them. She rolls her eyes and turns away from me, pissing me off even more.

"I just want to get Noah and go home."

"Answer me."

She shakes her head. "Just give me my son!" she yells, her hands instantly cover her face.

I can't, I won't. I will not hand over Noah without having the answers I want from her. I grab her arm and pull her into the house. She resists, fighting me as I drag her through the kitchen and down the stairs to my studio. It's a soundproof room so we can yell and scream at each other and Noah won't hear us.

I push her into the room and slam the door shut, locking it behind us.

"Who gave you these fucking papers, Josephine?" I hate saying her full name, but it gets her attention. She looks up at me, determined.

"You know, I thought we could work at this co-parenting thing, but I was wrong. I don't want your money, Liam. I don't need it. Noah and I have managed this whole time on our own so you don't have to worry about me sucking you dry."

"Josie –"

"No, let me finish." She holds up her hand, moving away from me, as far as she can get.

"No!" I yell at her. "I will not. Tell me who gave you these god damn papers. There is no postage so I know they were hand delivered. I'm really about to lose my shit here, so just tell me already."

"Why does it matter?"

"Because it's fucking bullshit!" I scream. "I didn't do this. I don't want this. I don't want to take Noah away from you or Beaumont."

I stalk over to her and push her up against the wall. My body is pressed against hers, as my hand cups her face gently. I want to do nothing more than to kiss her. To rip all her bulky winter layers away from her body and feel her skin against mine.

"I love our son, Josie. I love him so much. I would never do anything to hurt him and taking him away from you would do that." I try to calm down. I know who's behind this and for me this is the last straw.

"Her name is Sam," she says so quietly I almost don't hear her, but catching Sam escape from her lips is all the answer I need.

"Listen to me," I say, pulling her chin up so she's looking at me. "I bought this house with you in mind. I'm here because this is where my family is, you and Noah. I want to be with you.

"Sam's my manager and has clearly overstepped her boundaries. I don't know how she knows about Noah, but I'll find out. The last thing I want to do is to hurt you. I love you, Jojo."

"Please don't take him," she begs. I hate seeing her cry. I hate the look of desperation on her face. I'm going to kill Sam for doing this to Josie... to us. We don't need this drama in our lives.

I push a few strands of loose hair behind her ear. She leans into my touch, rubbing her cheek against my rough palm. I can't resist. I kiss away her tears until I find her mouth. I place three kisses along her lips, the first two in the corners before testing her reaction in the middle. She's receptive. Her hands pull me forward, closer.

I stop too soon for both of us. I want her, but not like this.

"Don't you want me?" she whispers against my lips.

"I do, so much, but not like this. Not in my studio where Noah can see us." I pull away from her and look into her beautiful blue eyes. "I want every part of you in my life, Jojo, when you're ready."

We walk back upstairs hand in hand, leaving the papers in my studio. I'll deal with them later. The first thing I need to do is call my lawyer and have them retracted. I don't even know what to do about Sam. Another question for my lawyer is if I can fire her? How much will it cost me to get out of this contract? She's gone too far this time.

NOAH and I start to set up the tree, centering it in front of the large picture window facing the street. Josie comes in, her face reserved. I know every expression she has and this one is hesitant, as if she's walking on egg shells. I need to fix this and fast.

I purposely slant the tree. When she huffs, I turn my head and hide my smile. She starts to boss us around, telling us right, left and finally throws her hands up when we don't listen to her. She leaves us men to the hard task of making our tree stand up right while she goes to the kitchen and works on making finger foods for tonight. Katelyn, the girls, Harrison and Quinn will be here shortly for our decorating party.

The Westbury men will have none of that. Noah and I sneak up on her in the kitchen. He tackles her from one side, and I the other. When she screams we start laughing. I can't help but kiss her. I hear Noah snicker and walk off, so I kiss her again. I know I shouldn't but I can't help it, I love her.

I kiss her a third time briefly on the lips when the front door bursts open. Katelyn yells to the girls to be respectful. Josie pushes me away. It should hurt my feelings but it doesn't. I know she wants to focus on Katelyn during the holidays. I make the decision to start wooing my girl. She needs to be romanced.

When Josie and I bring food into the living room, the kids, like vultures, attack right off. I leave them to answer the door. Harrison and Quinn are standing there, both holding out bouquets of flowers.

"You shouldn't have," I say, reaching for the flowers.

"Well, you are a sexy beast," Harrison says as he bats his eye lashes. I invite them in and direct them toward the festivities. Josie and Katelyn look up and smile when we enter.

"This is my Josie and our son, Noah." I point to Noah who looks up briefly and waves.

"Nice to meet you, Harrison. Hi Quinn," Josie says, bending down to his level.

Quinn waves as he inches closer to his dad, but hands Josie the bouquet of flowers.

"You know she's a florist, right?"

"Shut up, Liam. They're beautiful! Thank you, Quinn."
Josie eyes me like I'm in some sort of trouble. I sort of wish I
had taken advantage of her downstairs if she's going to look
at me like that.

"Harrison, this is our friend, Katelyn, and her daughters, Peyton and Elle." Both girls look up and smile before
they go back to sorting the ornaments.

Katelyn shakes Harrison's hand and in slow motion he
hands her the bouquet. She accepts the flowers, bringing
them in so she can inhale their scent. Her eyes look up at
him, his hand still holding the bouquet.

"Hi," he says as if he's just run five miles.

"Shit," I say, shaking my head. Josie looks from them to
me, her eyes going wide.

I pat Harrison on the shoulder and laugh. He lurches
forward before catching himself, never taking his eyes off of
Katelyn. Christmas just officially became interesting.

32

JOSIE

The smell of coffee wakes me. I bury my face into my pillow. The lingering scent of Burberry after shave weaves its way through my senses. Liam kissing me in his studio and again in the kitchen replays in my mind. I reach for him. I just need to feel him, to have his touch burning my skin knowing he's the only one who can extinguish the fire.

His side is empty and cold. I sit up suddenly. The bed covers are straight, untouched. His pillow is missing. I flop back onto mine and cover my face. I can't believe the simple smell of him can bring back such vivid memories.

"Are you sure we won't get into trouble?" I'm whispering even though he's assured me his parents are gone. Not just at work or the grocery store, but on a plane, heading for a cruise. How he convinced them to leave him home, I'll never understand, but I don't care because I get Liam all to myself.

He opens the door from the garage to the house. We stop in the kitchen briefly while he takes out two water bottles from the refrigerator. We climb the stairs hand in hand, until we reach his room. He hands me the water and pulls my silk scarf from my neck. Coming behind me, he places kisses along my neck before tying the scarf over my eyes.

"What are you doing?"

"Trust me," he says against my skin.

I do trust him. With my life.

He opens his bedroom door, his hands under my shirt, his fingers guiding me forward. His door slams shut causing me to jump. With my eye sight hindered my other senses are heightened.

Liam stands behind me, his breathing labored. When he moves away I want to follow him. Something clicks and the smell of cinnamon and something sweet, like cookies, permeates though the air.

He takes the bottles out of my hand and pulls me toward him. I stumble into him, my hands gripping his arms so I don't fall.

"I'll never let you fall, Jojo."

He brings me into the middle of his room, and into his arms. He caresses my cheek.

"I love it when you blush," he says huskily. His lips find mine, urgent with need, as he pulls the scarf loose. "Merry Christmas, my girl," he says as goose bumps spread across my skin. He picks me up, my legs wrapping around his waist as my hands tug at his clothes. He lays me gently on his bed, pulling away. I reach for him, causing him to laugh.

I look around the room. He's decorated it with Christmas lights and a small tree with a few presents underneath it.

"Which do you want to open first?" he asks.

"You," I say as I pull him down on top of me.

"Merry Christmas!" The door swings open and I'm greeted with the most beautiful sight in the world, my son and the man I am desperately trying not to love. I scoot up and attempt to straighten the rat's nest that has developed overnight.

Noah jumps up on the bed, with a small box in his hand. Liam follows, carrying a mug of coffee. He bends down as I reach for the cup and whispers 'Merry Christmas' into my ear. I want to pull him to me, just like the last time we were together at Christmas, but I refrain.

"This is for you," Noah shoves the small box toward me. I take a sip of my coffee before putting it down on the night stand. I don't know how I didn't notice the picture before, but there's Noah and I framed staring back at me. I don't know when Liam took the picture but it warms me knowing we're the first and last people he sees before going to sleep.

I smile at Liam who looks a little embarrassed. I'll be sure to ask him about it later. I take the gift out of Noah's hand and untie the large silky white bow. Noah scoots up next me while Liam sits just out of my reach.

I lift the lid on the black box. Nestled inside is a diamond heart-shaped pendant resting against crushed velvet.

"Look inside," Noah says giddily. Setting the box down, I slide my nail in between the ridge. It pops open easily and staring back at me is Noah and his toothless grin.

"You're supposed to be happy, not cry, Mom."

"I'm very happy, Noah. Thank you so much. I love it."

He reaches over and gives Liam a high-five. "You were right, Dad."

Noah jumps off the bed and heads for the door. "Come on, guys, Santa came!" Liam starts laughing and stares at the door until he's gone. As soon as he hears him downstairs he moves closer to me. He takes the box from my hand and removes the necklace. I lean forward, bending my head and wait for him to clasp the chain around my neck.

"Eager?" he asks. My eyes find Liam's, he's focused on me. I pull my hair to the side farthest away from him. He leans in, his scent enveloping me. His fingers linger on my skin following the path of the chain across my collarbone.

I turn my head slightly hoping to catch his lips. He doesn't disappoint. His lips brush against mine ever so lightly.

"Liam," I whisper. He pulls back and rubs his hand over his face. "What's wrong?"

"Nothing's wrong. I just don't want to rush this. I need you to be ready and not some rebound because you're hurting from Nick."

"But—"

"No buts. You were with him for a long time and things just ended. I'll be patient, Jojo." He stands and leans over me. I have to lean back so I can see him. "You will be mine again."

Once Liam is out of the room and my heart rate has returned to normal, I climb out of bed and change into something presentable. The moment I open the door, my name is being yelled from downstairs.

When I enter the living room seven pairs of eyes are staring at me. Apparently, I'm the last one to get out of bed this morning. One look at the tree and I see why everyone is ready. Santa came and brought the mall with him. I don't know where all this stuff came from, but whoever played Santa just made these kids' year.

Liam dons a Santa hat and passes out presents one by one. The look of elation spreads across his face when he reads his own name. He rips the paper off, causing the kids to laugh. The lid of the box goes flying and tissue paper rains down on us. He pulls out a photo album and starts flipping through the pages.

"Do you like it?" I ask him as his fingers ghost over ten years' worth of photos of Noah.

He stands and rushes over to me, picking me up. I wrap my arms around him, our faces buried in each other's necks. "Thank you so much," he mumbles against my neck. "I love it. I love it so much, Josie."

"I think your dad loves your mom," Quinn says to Noah. Harrison and Liam start laughing as do Katelyn and I.

Liam returns to his Santa duties, each child getting ample attention for each gift. I've held Katelyn throughout the morning. She occasionally wipes tears. Some are happy that Liam has made her girls' Christmas so special and others are for Mason.

After all the wrapping is thrown into the fireplace, Katelyn and I take to the kitchen to prepare dinner. The kids disperse throughout the house. Elle is with us while Peyton watches TV. The boys have gone outside to play with their new paintball guns while Liam and Harrison have retired to the studio to jam. I don't know what that means, but it makes Liam smile.

Once Katelyn and I finish preparing dinner, I cuddle on the couch with Peyton, while she and Elle snuggle up in the chair by the fire. When Liam comes up an hour later complaining that he and Harrison are hungry, I offer to make their lunch. He follows me into the kitchen, pulling at my hair.

"What are you doing?"

He walks toward me until I'm cornered. "I like seeing you comfortable in my house."

"Oh yeah?"

"Mhm. We need to go on a date."

"What happened to waiting and being patient?" I'm

losing whatever nerve I've told myself I need to keep around him. I want to be with him, but I also understand what he's saying about Nick. It's too soon, but I know what I want and it's Liam. I wanted him the day he walked into my shop.

I'm just scared.

Liam shrugs. He fingers the buttons on my shirt. "I will be patient, but I want to spend a lot of time with you."

"Okay."

"Yeah? How about New Year's Eve? Just us?" he's close enough to kiss. I lean forward only for his head to turn when the doorbell rings.

"You didn't invite your mom did you?"

"No, definitely not. I'll be right back." He kisses me on the cheek, leaving me frustrated and alone.

"Hey, baby." I freeze when I hear the same voice from the other day. I walk down the hall quietly.

"Sam, what the—"

"Oh my god," I gasp loudly as my hand covers my mouth.

33

LIAM

This has been the best morning I've had in a long time, from the moment when Noah and I woke up Josie with her gift to the unwrapping of mine. I can't wait to spend hours combing through every photo Josie gave me. Even though I'm not in them, having pictures of Noah when he was a baby, toddler and his first Halloween costume means everything to me.

I know I told Josie I can be patient, but I'm not sure I can. Seeing her in my bed, with her long dark hair spread across the pillow makes me want to claim her as mine. I knew I was a goner when I walked upstairs complaining about being hungry and she offered to make Harrison and I lunch.

Seeing her move around my kitchen like she owns it makes me want have her here every day, but I'm afraid. She was with Nick for a long time and you just can't turn off your emotions.

I should know.

I tried.

The sound of the doorbell saves me from making an

error in judgment. Swinging the door open, her back is facing me but I'd know that head of blonde hair anywhere. She turns and smiles as she steps in.

"Hey, baby," she coos. I swat at her hand when she tries to touch my face with her fake fingernails.

She just shrugs and opens her coat; she's clad in a barely-there bra and panties. Her stockings are held up by garters. At one time I found them sexy, but not so much anymore.

"Sam, what the—"

"Oh my god!"

I turn at Josie's gasp. The look on her face isn't anger, but hurt. She runs up the stairs, and the slamming of my bedroom door makes me jump.

"Cover yourself up. There are children in the house."

I walk away from her toward the dining room. I don't want her anywhere near the living room with Katelyn and the girls. Katelyn comes around the corner and motions that she's going upstairs. I nod and prepare for what I'm about to do.

"Sit down, Sam, we need to talk. And keep yourself covered."

I sit across from her. It's a safe distance so I won't hit her and she won't try and touch me. "I spoke to Brandon the other day."

"Me too," she says happily.

"This would be the day the mother of my son showed up demanding that I return her son to her."

"I took care of all that, baby."

"Sam, I'm not your baby and I'm never going to be. What you did was wrong on so many levels. I never doubted that Noah's mine. I also don't want custody. Josie wasn't some girl I met backstage; she was my girlfriend. How did you even know about Noah?"

She shrugs and starts looking at her fingernail. I know her game, this is the 'I have the answer but I'm not giving it' game. I slam my hand on the table to get her attention.

"I've been with your dad's agency since I started and never once have I questioned the integrity of his firm, but right now your job depends on it. I suggest you answer me."

"I didn't know you wanted him," she mumbles.

"What did you say?"

Sam rolls her eyes and sighs heavily. She's acting bored. "Someone claiming to know you called the agency when you first started. I put the messages in your file."

I bite the inside of my cheek, my hands clenching. "You knew I had a son and didn't tell me?"

"My dad said it was bad for your image."

"HE'S MY GOD DAMN SON!"

I get up and pace, my hands pulling at my hair. "She said she called and left messages. You took her calls and listened to her beg. Are you that much of a bitch, Sam? That woman calling you was my girlfriend and she was pregnant and scared and you ignored her. You kept my son from me. My god, how fucking heartless can you be?"

"Daddy did what was best."

"You're fired. I'm done with you. Get out of my house."

"Liam—"

"Don't," I hold up my hand for her to shut the hell up. "I said I'm done. I don't want you here."

"You need me."

"No, I don't. Get. Out."

"You heard him." I turn to find Josie leaning against the entry way. Her arms are crossed and she's been crying.

"This is our house and you need to leave. You're not welcome here."

"Is this what you want Liam?"

I can't help it. I smile at Josie and wink. "Yeah, she's the boss. If she says go, you go. Brandon will send you the separation agreement by the time you reach your car." I pull out my phone and text my lawyer to finalize the paperwork he started yesterday.

"You'll be sorry."

I step closer to her. "I'm already regretting the past ten years with you and your dad, so no, I won't be."

Sam gets up and walks to the door. She takes one look at me and shakes her head. I know she's about to cry and I don't care. As soon as the door closes, I pull Josie into my arms and hold her as if this is the last time I'm ever going to get the chance.

"I'm so sorry. I didn't know. I'm so very sorry for not being there for you," I tell her repeatedly. She strokes my hair, comforting me when I should be the one down at her feet groveling for forgiveness. With one single message all of this could have been avoided.

Katelyn and Harrison watch everything as it goes down. Harrison starts clapping when the door slams. I knew he was never a fan, but Sam made us money. Guess we'll have to figure that part on our own.

"Well, that was interesting," Katelyn says. Harrison looks down on her, his smile wide. I'm going to have to tell him to chill when it comes to Katelyn. "Just so you know, if you need a manager or something, I can probably help out for a bit."

"You're hired," Harrison blurts out causing Josie and I to laugh.

I shake my head and drag my friend away from his

newest obsession. Although, I guess if Katelyn is going to start dating ever again, Harrison would treat her right.

HARRISON and I emerge from the studio well after dark. He carries a sleeping Quinn upstairs, telling me goodnight along the way. I stay in the kitchen, ready to clean up the dinner mess. I told Josie and Katelyn I'd clean since they cooked a full dinner and dessert for everyone. When I flip on the light, however, there isn't a dish in the sink or on the counter. I look around and notice the small touches of Josie everywhere, fresh flowers on the windowsill, hand lotion by the sink and – the most obvious – our matching mom and dad mugs from Noah. They're sitting side by side next to the coffee pot, which is already set to go off in the morning. This means one thing.

She's planning on spending the night.

That means I'm sleeping on the couch.

I shut off the kitchen light and check the back door to make sure it's locked. I check the front door as well and turn off the remaining lights. I decide to leave on the candle lights that sit in the windows. I'm hoping Josie is still awake and maybe can talk.

We haven't really talked since before Nick left and I need to know where her head is. One moment she acts like she wants to be with me and the next she can't stand to be in the same room as me. I don't want to pressure her though, but I also don't want to sleep on the couch.

One concern I have, and shouldn't, is the relationship between Nick and Noah. Noah hasn't said anything about Nick leaving suddenly and has seen me kiss his mom. This is not the example I want to set for him. I want him to learn

boundaries and respect for women when they're in relation-
ships with other men. I have not done that with Josie. Of
course, Liam Page never cared. But Liam Westbury does.

Josie is sitting on the couch looking through my photo
album. Her legs are covered with her grandma's afghan, the
nameless cat curled up in her lap. There is a soft glow
around her, her dark hair being held back by the white
ribbon Noah used to wrap her necklace in. I lean against the
wall and watch her as she studies each page, every now and
again her face lifting in a smile.

"Are you just going to stand there and watch me?"

I push off the wall and walk toward her. She closes the
book and adjusts the way she's sitting. I take the spot next to
her and pull her legs into my lap, the cat hissing at me. She
laughs and sets him on the floor. "I like watching you. I have
a lot of time to make up for."

"Not with me," she replies softly.

"Yes, with you. I've missed so much. Like the day you
opened your flower shop or how you came up with the
name Whimsicality. I missed the day you brought Noah
into this world and saw him for the first time. I missed your
late-night cravings and his midnight feedings. I'll never
forgive myself for not being there, Josie. I won't. I know
you're about to tell me it's okay, but it's not. I trusted the
wrong people to take care of me when I'd left behind the
one person who would've taken care of me the best. I was
selfish and scared and instead of talking to you, I ran.

"But I promise you, I'm done running. I'm still selfish,
but only where you and Noah are concerned. I have years
of spoiling to make up for and I plan to spend every day of
my life making sure you both know how much I love you."

Josie wraps her fingers around mine. "I'm trying not to
love you. I'm telling myself that this is just a show for you, to

make Noah happy. I'm so afraid to show up one day and walk in and find that you've moved on because I've taken too long to make up my mind about us."

I knew she would feel like this, which is exactly why I didn't push myself on her.

"I've looked for you every day of my life since I left you in your dorm room. Every show, pub, or appearance I did – I thought for sure you'd show up somewhere. Not once, not even a glimpse. I desperately wanted to see you, just once. When I read about Mason, I knew I had to come. I told myself I'd show up and leave, in and out and no one would know I was here. But I ended up leaving a few days early because I wanted to see you just so I could tell myself I did the right thing."

"Why did you leave? You've never said?"

The dreaded question, the one I knew she shouldn't have to ask. I should've just told her the first day I saw her in her flower shop.

"When I got to college..." I shake my head feeling stupid. Now that I'm an adult, I would've done things differently. "God, Josie, it sucked. Mason was supposed to come with me. I mean we planned this and then he goes and changes his mind. I was there – he wasn't and you weren't. I was lonely and hated everything about it.

"This one day, I'm sitting in my room feeling sorry for myself and I get this call. She tells me her name is Betty Addison and I'm so confused until she tells me she's my grandma." I rub my thumb over the top of her finger. "She wanted to have lunch and talk so I did. I had nothing to lose and never had a chance to get to know her, so I met her. We spent a week together, having lunch, talking and getting to know each other. She told me things about my mom and why they don't speak to each other. I learned a lot in that week.

"She asked me what I wanted to be if I wasn't going to play football. 'What's your passion, Liam' she asked me. I told her music. I had been spending a lot of time on campus at open mic and I loved it."

"I wish I had known that you loved music that much."

"You had this dream and I didn't want to change that for you. I was doing what was expected, but Betty – she invited me to Los Angeles so I went and loved it. I knew I had made the best decision for me even though it meant destroying us.

"Thing is, I never expected to see Noah in the bathroom that day, but it was like fate or some shit telling me that my life is in Beaumont. I went right to your shop and waited. I watched for you and once I saw you, I knew I was going to end up chasing my girl, waiting for you to turn around and see... the real me and love me for who I am and not what I did to you.

"I'm standing in front of you, Josie. You just have to turn around."

34

JOSIE

I could easily fall into a routine with Liam. How soon is too soon though? Is there a rule book I need to follow?

Liam and I have never shared a home. We didn't go off to college together and have the opportunity to sleep in each other's dorms. Being here – it's peaceful - sharing the same space that he's in. Almost like the walls bask in his presence.

I haven't left since Christmas. We didn't discuss me staying. I just stayed. I guess that makes me a bit like Nick. For the first few nights he slept on the couch or in his studio until I couldn't stand it anymore. I finally found the nerve to pull him upstairs with me and into bed. He held me all night, his hands never once wandering away from their placement on my hip.

We're apparently keeping things platonic even though I know he wants me and I want him.

I'm dreading the return to my house. School starts back up in a few days and while this has been a nice vacation, reality is pushing itself back into my life. I caught Liam and Harrison discussing a possible move to Beaumont. I know that would make me happy because that means Liam isn't traveling back and forth all the time to work. And I think Harrison has a crush on Katelyn. There is no mistaking he has eyes for her and watching him with the twins during Christmas, as much as I hate to say it, I know Mason would approve.

Tonight, Liam has promised me a night filled with debauchery. He says we've missed far too many New Year's Eves. When I asked him what the night will entail, he just smiled and walked away. I'd be lying if I said I it wasn't driving me crazy not knowing his plans.

With Noah packed and in the car, the drive over to my parents' is nerve-wracking. They haven't been too impressed with Liam's return, not that I can blame them. Because of his involvement with Noah, my parents have been in the shadows. It's not that I don't want them around, but under the circumstances I thought it best to let Liam get to know Noah without my parents stringing him up on a burning stake.

I can't blame my parents for their feelings. They were the ones who had to pick up the pieces and take care of their pregnant, teenage daughter. My mom was there, holding my hand, when I delivered Noah when it should've been Liam. My parents are bitter, I get that, but people can change.

This will be the first time seeing my parents since Thanksgiving. They just returned from a holiday cruise. I told them about Nick over an email. Not necessarily the way I wanted to tell my parents that my boyfriend of six years has left, but I also didn't want them to find out through town gossip.

My dad is waiting for us on the porch when we pull into the driveway. Noah jumps out of the car before I have it turned off and runs into his arms. If Noah wasn't nine I'd say he's excited about seeing his grandparents, but I have a feeling it's more about the second Christmas he's about to have.

I carry an armload of presents into the house. I love the smell of my parents' home, the fresh baked bread, pies and cakes always coming out of my mother's oven gives their house a welcoming and the all-over home feel.

"Merry Christmas and Happy New Year," I say as I enter. My parents are already sitting on the couch listening to Noah rattle on about everything he received for Christmas and his new friend, Quinn.

Each time he mentions Liam's name, my dad glares at me. I knew things would be a bit on edge, but honestly it's my life and I made the best decision for me and my son. I should be respected and not made to believe I've done something wrong.

After we've caught up, presents are handed out. Noah is buried under the mountain of gifts my parents bought him.

"Can I start?" he asks. My dad laughs and tells him to start ripping. I don't like Christmas this way, it's too fast and you miss what's being opened. I keep my stack of presents, all sweaters, skirts and scarves, the same as every year, on the floor and watch Noah.

"Oh, cool! A remote control car. My dad is going to love this."

My dad grunts and stalks out of the room. I get up and follow him into the kitchen. His hands grip the edge of the counter as he mutters to himself.

"Dad," I say touching his shoulder. He stands and looks at me with sadness in his eyes. "I know you're upset about Liam, but you can't let Noah see or hear you like that. He doesn't know anything other than Liam being his dad. He's trying really hard to build a relationship with Noah and we need to support it. I know you don't like it, but I need you to put on a game face for your grandson."

"He's going to hurt you, Josephine."

I shake my head. "He's not, dad."

"You don't—"

"I do, I can feel it. Things are different. He didn't know about Noah. You should've seen his face when he found out. I knew right then that he would've been here, daddy. I know it in my heart."

I pull my dad into my arms and hold him. He's been my rock for so long. I know he's afraid that Liam is going to run for the hills, but I have to trust my heart with this one.

The rest of the afternoon goes well even though each time Noah mentions Liam, my dad fights a grimace and plasters on some sort of smile. I can't imagine how he feels. He was there when I needed him most, but I now need Liam.

Noah also needs Liam. He needs his dad and even though he had Nick, I can't deny the instant bond Liam and Noah have. It was evident the first time I saw them together. Noah knew Liam was his dad and treated him as such without calling him out. I know I'm making the right decision.

I kiss Noah goodbye after we eat an early dinner. I promise to pick him up tomorrow afternoon for our annual college football party at Katelyn's. My parents don't ask me what my plans are for tonight, but as I'm leaving my dad whispers for me to be careful.

Driving back to my house seems surreal. When I open the door, it's cold and uninviting. For the first time I look at the walls and think they are drab and in need of a serious paint job even though I just painted them in the spring.

Everything feels as if it's lacking life. I know that if I want to be with Liam, I need to show him. Words aren't going to be enough, not for him at least. He needs to feel it in his heart that I'm committed to him. He wants us to be a family and I want that too. I don't want to spend any more nights away from him.

I've been waiting since I was fifteen to have the opportunity to wake up in his arms day after day. So what if we had a ten-year road block? The opportunity is here now and I need to take it.

I take a quick shower, careful not to get my hair wet so I can curl the ends. Tonight I've opted for a royal blue one-shoulder metallic dress. Katelyn and I found it at an after Christmas sale that was too good to pass up. My hands shake as I apply my make-up. I mess up too many times to count and have to start over. The last time I was this nervous was my first date with Liam. Of course any girl is a bundle of nerves when they're going to their first major dance, but it was more for me then and it's the same now.

I want everything to be perfect.

I wash my face and start over, climbing up onto the counter because I can barely stand without having my knees shake. I slip in my ear buds and turn on some soothing music. With deep calming breaths, I focus on making my eyes smoky.

It takes me longer than usual to fix my make-up and hair. I pin my hair to the side, away from the shoulder that is going to be exposed. My tear-drop diamond earrings are in and I'm ready for my dress. That is what I tell myself as I stand in front of my closet staring at it while it mocks me. What if he doesn't like the dress? What if he thinks I'm trying too hard? Maybe I should just wear jeans and cowboy boots. He's always liked that look.

But that was before he went to Hollywood and became famous and had women – gorgeous beautiful women throwing themselves at him. In dresses much shorter no less. I shake my head to try and get the image out of it and give myself a pep talk. I can't think like this because if I do, I know I'll be a nervous wreck by the time I arrive at Liam's. Removing my outfit carefully from the hanger, I step into it, shimmying until I can push my arm into the sleeve.

I step into my peep toe heels and take deep breath before looking in the mirror. I stand there with my eyes closed and imagine Liam staring at me. In my mind, he's smiling as his eyes wander over my body. He's remembering what I feel like under his touch and how his lips make my body sing to him. He'll pull me to him and carry me upstairs, our night forgotten because he knows I'm ready.

Ready for him and no one else.

My palms sweat. My body is flushed. I open my eyes and stare at the woman in the mirror. Staring back is a girl I once knew, one that shined and sparkled every time she was about to go see her boyfriend. This girl looks happy.

I try not to speed while driving back to Liam's. I'm anxious and my heart is racing. My hands slip repeatedly from the steering wheel. My foot misses the gas one too many times. I'm a danger to the people on the road, but I can't hurry. My mind is clouded with thoughts of me under Liam as he makes love to me. I need to make Liam want me as desperately as I want him.

Liam is at the door before I can set my hand on the knob. I swallow hard when I see him. He's dressed from head to toe in black. His shirt sleeves are rolled, showing off the tattoos on his forearms. I lick my lips in anticipation of being able to trace each one with my mouth. He's wearing a black leather bracelet on his right wrist and a watch on the other. Both of which I want to take off so he's free of any obstacles when I finally get to touch him. His blue eyes darken as he looks at me. When he licks his lips, I go weak in the knees and have to balance myself by holding onto the door jam.

I don't know if my date is with Page or Westbury, but I think tonight I'd like to go out with Liam Page.

I pull the door open before she has a chance to open it. My day has been utter shit with her gone. I don't know how I grew accustomed to her being here so quickly, but I did. Waking up next to her these past few days has been beyond words. Holding her in my arms, while she sleeps and feeling her body against mine, indescribable. Many times I've wanted to take her, claim her as mine, but I've held back. I need to do this right. I'm just not sure how much longer I can hold out. She's a temptress and she's calling my name.

I drink her in, every inch of her toned body. There was a time in my life when I was allowed to explore her freely, where she'd beg for me to touch her. I want to relive those memories and make them my reality.

Her heels are shorter than most women wear. I like this. It allows me to pull her close and look down at her, which I plan to do all night. Her legs are bare, leading to the dress I know she picked up with Katelyn and teased me about. Visions of my hands going under the hem, grabbing her ass and pulling her to me flood my mind. I have to close my eyes for a minute to clear my thoughts because if I don't, we aren't leaving this house. It's empty tonight and I don't have any qualms about taking advantage of that.

Her little dress is one of those one-shoulder things, giving me ample opportunity to place my lips all over her shoulder and neck. Not that a sleeve or strap would've stopped me, but with this much freedom I may not need a cocktail to ring in the New Year. I'll be drunk off her.

There is no one sexier than the woman standing before me.

I contemplated tonight for a few days. I didn't know where to take her. Half of me wanted to take her to Los Angeles and show her off. I've been invited to a few parties for tonight and any one of them would grant me the ability to parade her around. But that means paparazzi and I'm not sure she's ready or realizes what it's going to mean to be with me. When I think about her picture spread all over the gossip rags, it makes me sick. I need to hire someone to handle the public side of my life now that I've fired Sam.

I decided to take her to Ralph's. Tacky, I know, but its close and if we decide to drink we can walk home. Although, with the way she's looking tonight, we may make a pit stop in a few, very well-known backyards.

Her eyes sparkle when she smiles. I reach for her hand, pulling her into the house. There is so much I want to ask her and yet words seem so futile right now, especially when we can communicate with our bodies. I reach out and run my fingers lightly through her hair, brushing her long bangs away from her face. She sighs when I cup her cheek. I fight the urge to lean down and kiss her. Once I do, our night will escalate and I want to enjoy her. I want to take her on a date. I'm a selfish man. I want heads to turn when I walk in with her on my arm.

"God, you're gorgeous," I say quietly.

"You're so fucking hot." Her eyes go wide as she covers her mouth. I pull her hand away from her mouth.

"You think so?"

"Don't be cocky."

My reaction is to pull her close and let her feel what she does to me. Her eyelids flutter, causing me to close my eyes. With my forehead against hers, my hands trail over her ass. Her breathing stills when I push her into me. Her tiny gasp sends waves of heat through my body. If I don't let go, I'm going to take her right here on the floor.

I promised her a date.

I step away from her reluctantly. Her eyes shimmer with want. I definitely plan to deliver. I take her hand in mine and lead her out of the house. I need the fresh air and a crowded place otherwise I'm not going to make it through the night without stripping her bare or at least hiking up that dress of hers.

In the car I place her hand on my thigh. It's a mistake. I have a feeling tonight will be a long list of mistakes. Her fingers brush against me each time I shift. And I'm finding a lot of reasons to shift.

I feel her stiffen when we pull into Ralph's. The excitement that was evident on the way here is gone. She's upset.

I lean over and pull her face to mine, my lips meeting hers. She softens against me. I hold her to me, my hand cupping her face.

"It's not what you expected?"

"No, it's fine." She turns away from me, her hands rubbing down the front of her dress. Her earlier smile now masked by indifference.

"I wanted to take to you L.A. There are all these parties and I know you'd have a good time, but I wouldn't be able to keep my hands off of you and the paparazzi would be all over you." My finger traces the top of her dress. "I wanted to give you all of my attention tonight." She looks down at my finger as it caresses the swell of her breasts.

She looks at me.

"I don't want to share you, Jojo. That day is going to come soon enough, probably sooner than we think. I just want one night where I can hold you, dance with you and touch you without people being in my face about it."

"The last time you were here people took your photo," she reminds me.

I turn away from her and follow a group of people into Ralph's. I never expected her to want the glitz and glamour that my life offers. I should've asked her what she wanted before bringing her here. Maybe I should've known she'd want a taste of the celebrity life. Hell, I denied her the opportunity once before; maybe I should throw her into it.

"Josie I can give you anything you want, but I can't offer you peace and quiet all the time. We've been lucky with the paparazzi. You know I'm having a gate installed and a concrete fence because I want our home to be private. I want Noah to be able to play outside. We need security. I don't want to give up who I am, but I want a life with you and tonight I want it to be here in our hometown because next year I could be on tour or we could be at a party someplace. I just want one night."

"Which Liam am I out with tonight?"

I smirk. I never thought I'd hear that question come out of her mouth. "I wasn't aware there were two."

"There definitely are."

"Hmm... well which one do you want?" My voice is deep, dangerous. I'm tempting her, waiting for her answer even though I know what she's going to say.

"Page," she answers seductively.

"You want the rock star, the bad boy?"

She nods.

Who am I to deny her?

I get out of the car, slamming the door. I hesitate, looking at her shadow in the front seat. Liam Page would never have a woman in his car, let alone open a door for her, but she's my girl. I step to her side and open the door for her. I can't help but gawk at her legs as she steps out of the car, her hand in mine. I kiss her briefly before pulling her behind me into Ralph's.

Inside, the place is packed. Ralph brought in a DJ for the night in hopes of increasing business. He's definitely done that. Josie and I hit the bar first. I order us each a drink. Whiskey for me and some fruity ass drink for her. Ralph says hi and tells me he has a reserved table for us. Not something I wanted, but I'll take it as there's no place to sit.

Leading Josie through the crowd of people, my name is shouted – women look at me with lust in their eyes and people slap me on the back. Word has spread that this is my hang out. Good for Ralph. Bad for me.

Our booth is in a dark corner, which I like. Josie slides in first and I follow, sitting as close as I can to her. I drape my arm over her shoulder, sliding my fingers under the top of her dress. Her hand is on my thigh, stroking my leg. If she keeps that up, we won't be here very long.

She looks at me, her eyes full of anticipation. I hate what I'm about to do to her, but she asked for it.

I lean, my nose running along her jaw until I get to her ear. I bite down gently. Hearing her gasp urges me on. I suck her earlobe into my mouth. My hand trails up her leg, pushing her thighs slightly apart.

"Is that what you do on a date?" she asks, eagerly.

"I don't date," I reply quickly.

"Ever?" she asks as her voice breaks. I kiss my way toward her mouth before answering.

"I fuck." I capture her lips with mine before she can say anything. Her lips and tongue react immediately to mine. My fingers reach her panties. They're silk. And wet. I pull my hand away and stop kissing her.

I can't sit here in this booth with her like this, willing to let me do things in public. I grab her hand and pull her out to the dance floor. I want more for us when we're together again.

"Did I do something wrong?" she asks close to my ear. She has to yell over the music.

I shake my head. "I don't know if I can be Liam Page around you. He doesn't treat women very well."

She answers me by grinding against me, urging me on, showing me she doesn't care. God, I love her but we can't happen like this.

Purple Rain comes on. It's the song we first danced to at homecoming. It's perfect for us. I wrap my arms around her waist, my hands resting on her ass. She places her hands in my hair. Closing my eyes I let the music move us, guide us. I want her to feel her effect on me. She needs to know that I want her, that my body is craving her.

I open my eyes and look down at the woman who holds all my fantasies. Her finger traces the outline of my lip before she leans in and shows me how much she wants me. We make out like the horny teenagers we once were, in a bar full of people we used to know.

I want to live in these arms. They make me feel secure, loved, needed. His hands don't roam. They stake their claim and hold me tight to his body. He leads us on the dance floor in a sinful tangle of gyrating hips. His eyes are dark and seductive. I'm done allowing him to question my state of mind. I vow to make him mine.

The song changes, but we don't move. It's like the DJ knows we want to be close. Not that we'd stop what we're doing. I rest my head on his shoulder, my body keeping rhythm with his. I don't know how I've forgotten what it feels like being with him like this. I used to count the days until our next dance just so I could hold him.

I place small kisses on his neck. He grips me tighter and nuzzles my ear. My hand finds the top button of his shirt. I play with the button until it opens. His hand stills mine, pulling it away from his shirt. I'd pout if he could see my face fully. He sets my hand on his chest, just over his heart and holds it there as his lips touch mine softly.

He pulls away abruptly and looks over his shoulder. A woman comes into view. Her hair is piled on top of her head in a messy 'I don't give a shit' bun. Her skin-tight red dress is showing so much of her breasts. Liam doesn't have to imagine what they look like. She licks cherry red lips and she looks at Liam like he's taking her home tonight.

"Can I have this dance?" she asks brazenly. Can't she see he's with someone?

"I'm kind of busy." He turns back to me. His expression telling me he's sorry we were interrupted.

"How about an autograph or a picture?"

Liam rolls his eyes. Apparently she doesn't get it. She pulls her cell phone out of the top of her dress and hands it to me. I look at Liam, my eye brow raised. If he thinks I'm touching that phone he's nuts, let alone take a picture of them together.

"No pictures, not tonight. I'm on a date."

"Maybe we can meet up later?"

Before I can say anything, Liam says, "I'm on a forever kind of date so no thanks."

She looks annoyed and glares at me. Sorry chick, he's mine. If I have to wear a shirt claiming him, I will. She pulls out a tube of lipstick and spins it until the bright red is showing.

"Sign here." She runs her finger over the top of her breasts.

Liam shakes his head. "Paper or nothing," he says turning back to me and pulling me into his arms. I can't help but throw her a knowing look and smile as I hold onto his shoulders. She stands there, her leg pointed out like she's just waiting for another opportunity to pounce on my man.

We only sit for a little bit before more people come up and bug him, asking for photos or autographs. Women bring him drinks, but he pushes them aside. He tells me that he never accepts drinks from anyone because that's how

Harrison ended up with Quinn. He met this woman back-stage and woke up at her place. Nine months later she dropped off Quinn. I can't image leaving Noah. He's my life and for the longest time my only reminder of what Liam and I had.

Liam takes me back to the dance floor. He requests a series of songs from the DJ, most are his. Songs that I've memorized and know are about me, our love and the things he wants to do to me.

When the clock strikes twelve his lips claim mine, solid and confident, like he's been waiting for this moment forever. I know I have.

"Are you ready to get out of here?" he says against my lips. He doesn't wait for an answer. He pulls me through the cheering crowd. When we're outside he rushes us to the car. He pushes me up against it, and wraps my legs around him. I feel him fumbling for the door. The leather is cold against my skin as he sets me down in the seat. "Hold that thought."

Liam climbs into the car and starts it. He places my hand on his hard on, sighing when I squeeze him lightly. He pulls out of the parking lot, gravel spitting out behind the car and drives us home as fast as he can.

My nerves are on fire when we pull into the driveway. I haven't moved my hand and yet I feel as if this is our first time all over again. Except this time we're in his house, not a hotel. I let myself out of the car and meet him around the front. We walk hand in hand into the dark house. Only the candles in the window light a path through the darkness.

He bends, placing one arm under my legs, the other behind my back. He takes the steps slowly, his eyes pene-trating mine. I can see the desire, feel it in the way he holds me. He pushes the bedroom door open, kicking it shut when we're inside.

He sets me down on his bed and stands in front of me, pushing my hair off my shoulder. He kneels letting his hands trail down my legs, sending a shiver over my skin. He picks up each foot and removes my shoes. His fingers dance along my skin until he reaches the hem of my dress. I stand, forcing him to take a half step back.

My hands slide up his covered chest, fingers working the buttons. I'm so eager to see his chest, one that I've missed for so many years. I close my eyes when I get to the last button, my hands pushing aside the fabric. I allow my hands to explore feeling the tight ridges of his abs as my fingers memorize every plane. His hands clamp down on mine when I get to his chest.

"Open your eyes."

When I do, he lets go. He wanted to see my eyes when I finally discovered what he's been hiding. On his left pec there's ink and lots of it. It's dark, solid black. My finger outlines the edges, following the maze.

"What's this?"

"It's a tribal design," he answers without hesitation. "Trace here," he says as he moves my fingers along his tattoo. I do as he asks, my mind telling me what my heart already knows.

"It says—"

"It says, Jojo." I place an open mouth kiss over my name. He pulls at my hips. I can feel him, his need evident through his jeans. He's been this way all night, waiting patiently to get us back here so we can finally be together.

Liam turns me around, wrapping his arm around my waist. He rubs his hard on against the swell of my ass. I can't help but push into him. He pushes my dress off my shoulder, his lips pressing against the exposed skin. I tilt my head, resting on his shoulder as his hands rub over my breasts. My hand reaches back, weaving through his hair. He moves away from me, lips burning a trail down my back. Fingers tug at my dress, pushing it down my legs. I'm bare except for the thong I'm wearing. I feel his teeth pull at the side of my panties. I turn. I need to see him, touch him.

He picks me up and lays me on the bed, crawling over me. I arch up to feel his skin on mine. I drag my fingers through his hair. He looks at me, breathing shuddered. The intensity of his gaze makes my skin tingle in anticipation. His thumb brushes under the curve of my breast.

He sits back, undressing. I sit up and rub my hand over his chest, abs and finally his bulge. His eyes roll back in his head as I touch him. He crawls over me, pushing me back into the mattress. I wrap my arms around his shoulders, urging him. He settles on me, his weight and heat a welcome feeling.

"I love you, Jojo," he says against my lips. He holds my hands above our heads, his forehead touching mine. Our mouths drops open in ecstasy, remembrance as he moves, working his body into mine. I cry out, grasping at his hands. My legs move over his hips, guiding and holding him where I need him most.

I moan as he flexes his hips, going deeper. I can't stop looking at him, his eyes watching me, relearning how good we are together. When he lets go of my hands, I dig into his ribs, encouraging him to move faster.

Liam moves to his knees, moving my body by the push and pull of my legs. "I need to look at you," he says breathlessly.

My hands clamp down on his forearms, hanging on as he moves us in rhythm. He drops my legs, moving to kiss me. He makes love to my mouth while he moves faster, harder, bringing me to the edge.

"Liam!" I need more.

He knows my body and grunts just as my orgasm takes over. My toes curl, my nails dig into his ass as I lift my hips to meet his last thrusts.

He stills, collapsing on top of me. I lay there, my muscles weak and tired, yet completely satisfied and ready to do this again. I stroke his back, causing him to shiver. I kiss his neck, his cheeks and finally lips.

"I love you, Liam. I love you so much."

He looks at me and smiles. He leans on his elbow, not moving from where he's nestled between my legs. He could stay there forever for all I care. He moves my damp hair away from my face and kisses my nose.

"Move in with me? You and Noah move here and we'll be a family. I want you to call this your home. I want to do normal things with you like go grocery shopping and meet you for lunch at work."

"That's sounds like the American dream."

"No, my girl, that's our dream. If you want it, I'll give it to you."

"I want it."

Liam's smile lights up the dark room. We kiss for a while before he rolls over and pulls me on top of him.

"**S**on, come down here."

My eyes roll automatically when he speaks to me these days. I never thought I'd cringe at the sound of my father's voice, but I do. The closer I get to graduation, the more of a hard ass he's become.

The day I asked Josie to homecoming the dissension started. My parents sat me down and explained the concept of socially acceptable standards. In a nutshell, Josie isn't country club enough to be seen with a Westbury.

For the first time I saw my parents in a different light. I was disgusted to be their son. I couldn't understand how they could say something so horrible about someone they didn't even know. The night of homecoming I walked out of my house in my tux without saying goodbye or allowing my mom to take a picture. I wasn't going to let them dictate who I dated, or who I loved for that matter.

"I'll call you back," I say to Josie. She doesn't come over anymore. She gave up a long time ago. She even offered to break up with me so my life would be easier. I told her no way in hell was I going to let Sterling and Bianca Westbury drive her away.

Josie is the best thing to ever happen to me. She understands me.

Throwing my phone on the bed, I sigh. I'm counting the days until I'm out of here. Mason and I are taking the girls camping for a week before we leave for college. One last hurrah and a week of pure solitude for me and Josie. No annoying parents looming over our shoulder.

When I get downstairs, I'm greeted by an ominous look from my father. He's up to something. He pats me on the shoulder and leads me into the living room. There sitting on the couch, with her legs crossed, is his golfing buddy's daughter, Sasha.

I groan and rub my hands over my face. In this position I could elbow my dad in the gut and run for it, but Sasha has already seen me and is standing, walking toward me with her hand out as if I'm to kiss it. Like I owe her a thank you for being in my house. No thanks.

"Liam, it's so good to see you." Her voice is whiney, nasally. I can't stand it. I grimace which only makes her smile brighter. Her teeth are so white. She could light a dark street at night.

"Sasha," I say coldly, uninterested.

"Well, I thought you two could come with us tonight," Sterling says. Again with the eye rolling which Sasha witnesses.

"Or we could stay in," she offers.

I recoil at the thought of spending time with her. "I have plans."

"Oh, I don't mind hanging out with you and your friends." She laughs as her hand trails down my arm. I move away, offended by her touch.

I don't remember offering I want to blurt out. "I'm sure you don't, but my girlfriend does," I say just so I can goad Sterling. He stiffens and I want to laugh. His matchmaking is failing which means his buddy is going to be pissed.

"Excuse us for a moment, Sasha." My dad grabs my arm and pulls me into the other room. I'm about to get a tongue lashing, something I may thoroughly enjoy.

"Liam, it's about time you look at your future. You're going away to college and Sasha is a fine woman to have on your arm, especially when the NFL scouts you. You need to present the full package and she completes that. You can't have riff raff from across the tracks hanging on just so she has someone to support her."

His words fuel nothing but pure anger. "You don't know shit about Josie and her family." I point at him, pushing my finger into his chest. "You do nothing but sit on your pompous ass and look down on people who don't go to your stupid ass country club. I love her and I plan to marry her whether you like it or not. If you want some arm candy, why don't you date Sasha? She's probably looking for a sugar daddy anyway."

"Where are you going?" he asks as I walk away.

"Out with my friends. It's Mason's birthday so you'll have to entertain Sasha. Just don't let mom catch you." I slam the door effectively cutting him off.

I shake my head to clear away that memory. I've hated my dad for so long for the way he's treated Josie. Even though my mom comes around to see Noah, I refuse to step foot into their house. She's trying. I'll give her that, but him... no way. If he couldn't accept Josie in my life back then, I'll be damned if I'm going to allow him anywhere near my son.

So much has changed in the past four months. Josie and

Noah moved into my – our – house after New Year's. Harrison and Quinn have also moved to Beaumont and right into Josie's empty house. Which I knew was going to happen. It all made sense. That also put him in the same neighborhood as Katelyn, where, if you drive by on Saturday, you see him and his tattooed arms mowing her lawn.

Tonight we're celebrating Mason's birthday. It's been seven months since he left us and we've each struggled and coped differently. We held our fundraiser for Katelyn and the girls at Ralph's, which has become a local hotspot, and did fairly well. I've also hired Katelyn as my manager effectively giving her a stay at home job, even though she has to come to my house and work every day. As soon as school is out for the summer we're heading out on tour. Three band members, two bossy women and four kids touring for three months. Band life will be different now.

I'm waiting for Josie to get ready. My truck, a recently acquired nineteen sixty-five Chevy, is strictly for water tower drinking. When I told Josie about my purchase, she slapped me in the arm and told me to grow up. Yet she's the first one to yell for a 'water tower' night when we're in need of a reality check.

I load the back of the truck with a cooler full of beer. Josie will be our designated driver tonight, which I'm thankful for. I want tonight to be fun and somewhat enjoyable for Katelyn. Josie walks out of the house, her arms full of food. I run over to her, kissing her on the cheek and relieving her of the heavy load. We had the food catered as I didn't want Josie or Katelyn stressing about what people will eat.

I turn back and look at her after putting everything into the back of the truck. I take in her appearance. She's dressed in tight jeans with her red cowboy boots. Her tight, 'I love my rocker' tank top hugging her curves nicely. She dresses like this to tease me.

I saunter over to her and sweep her into my arms, bending her backward and attacking her neck. She giggles and tries to push me away with her head. She finally relents, knowing I've won.

I set her back on her feet. "Ready?" I ask. She nods, threading her fingers into mine. She climbs into the truck through the driver's door, settling in the middle. Just like in high school.

When we arrive at the water tower, there are a bunch of people here. I was surprised when Katelyn said she wanted to invite people from high school, but went along with it. Josie and I hop out of the truck, hand in hand. I drop the tailgate and help her set up. Harrison comes over to say hi before snagging a beer out of the cooler.

"I'm going to head up, okay?" I kiss her on the cheek and pocket a few beers. Mason's truck is lined up just perfectly for our beer torpedoes. Harrison follows me up the ladder. Most of the guys already at the tower know him, but I make a few introductions.

We pop open our first beer and chug. On the count of three, we throw our bottles down. With the loud crash of glass shattering we all yell out 'Mason!' The women start cheering and the music is turned up.

We start the party in true Mason style.

As the night goes on, stories are told and retold. The comfortable camaraderie that we all had in high school is back. I'm no longer the asshole that ditched everyone and Harrison fits in with everyone. I'm literally living the best of both worlds and I couldn't be happier.

I look at Harrison when I hear him sigh heavily.

"What's wrong with you?"

"Nothing," he says. I follow his gaze and see that Katelyn's talking to Bill Rogers, some geek turned millionaire for creating a computer program that everyone loves.

Bringing my bottle of beer to my lips, I look back at Harrison. His expression is sad. I know he likes her but is afraid of being turned down.

"Take your time with Katelyn, man. Just be there and don't push her. They were together for a long time, but I know she notices you. I've heard her talking to Josie about you. Just seize the moment when it's there."

Harrison starts laughing. "You're one to talk."

"What the hell are you talking about?"

"You write song after song about how much you love that woman." He points to Josie who's talking to Jenna. "You live with her, share a son, yet I don't see you asking her to marry your sorry ass."

I look from Josie to him and back again.

"You're right." I stand up, holding on the railing, place my fingers through my lips and whistle loudly getting everyone's attention.

"Hey, Josie!"

"What do you want, Westbury?" she yells back. I love how some things haven't changed.

"Will you marry me?"

Someone kills the music and silence spreads over the field. She moves closer to the water tower and sets her hands on her hips. "If you're going to ask me, you better do it proper."

"Yes ma'am." I down my beer and toss it toward the truck and make my way to the ladder. I climb down carefully. When my feet hit the ground I pat my pocket for the ring I've had in there for the past few weeks and pull it out, keeping it in my palm. I've just been waiting for the right moment. This must be it.

I stroll over to her, my steps wide so I'm there faster. Her hands are still on her hips, her eyes wide. She's not expecting this.

I bend down on one knee in front of her. Her hand goes to her mouth and there's a collection of gasps behind us.

"Josie Preston I have loved you since I was sixteen. I know I've screwed up a whole lot, but I promise to make it up to you every day. Would you do me the immense honor of wearing my ring, taking my name and becoming not only my partner in life, but most importantly, my wife?"

Josie nods. There are tears in her eyes and I want to get up and kiss them away. "Yes, Liam. Yes a million times over I'll marry you."

I pull her hand forward and slide the ring on, kissing her finger before I kiss her. There is loud applause and cheering behind us.

"I love you, Jojo. You're forever my girl."

ACKNOWLEDGMENTS

To say this has been a whirlwind journey is an understatement. When I started, I never thought I'd get this far. To hold my book, to see my name in print and to hear about people reading something I wrote is all too surreal.

Yvette Rebello ∼ No words will ever capture what you mean to me. This adventure, it's not possible without your guidance and support. I can't imagine ever doing this without you. Thank you for putting up with all my crazy story ideas and being the sounding board that I needed.

Holly Stephens ∼ To have you be on this ride is a tremendous honor. I will always remember the story that brought us together and how it's guided and allowed us to develop an everlasting friendship. I'm excited to be starting this process with you.

Forever My Girl would not be possible without Yvette & Holly. The countless hours of emails, text message and phone calls shaped the cast of characters that make up Forever My Girl. I am and will always be in their debt.

Eric Heatherly ∼ Without you, your lyrics and music, Liam doesn't come alive. You've given me an opportunity to bring something different to my novels and for that I thank you.

Cari Renee ∼ Thank you, from the bottom of my heart, for helping bring Liam alive on stage. If it wasn't for your love of music, Cari, I would've never been introduced to Eric. I'm forever grateful.

Jillian Dodd ∼ How can I ever say thank you enough for everything that you've done for me? From answering rambling and incoherent text and email messages to holding my hand and helping me build a fan base. I'm so proud to be representing Bandit Publishing. Thank you for the opportunity.

Damaris Cardinali ∼ What started as a risk when I sent you Forever My Girl has turned into a great friendship. I can't thank you enough for your support and the support Good Choice Reading Reviews has given me.

Beth Suit ∼ Wow. Thanks to Jillian we met and for that I'm so thankful. You have been a true blessing to have in my life. Thank you so much for all your hard work on Forever My Girl. I look forward to a long and fulfilling friendship with you.

Sarah Hanson ∼ To say I'm in awe of your talent would be an understatement. What you did, bringing Forever My Girl to life, amazing. I will never be able to thank you enough, nor will I be able to look at my gorgeous cover and not cry.

Fallon Clark ∼ Thank you for always being there when I need your red pen.

And finally to my family. Erik, Madison & Kassidy ∼ thank you for putting up with me always being in the other room, sitting with my laptop while we watch TV and the late nights. Your support, guidance and encouragement means more to me than I can ever tell you. Mom; Dad &

Beth – look at what I did! Nicole & Becky: Thank you for reading and giving me feedback. Jenn Sy: your encouragement knows no bounds.

Jen Howell: you had the first official ARC & review, I couldn't have asked for a better person to give Liam too.

Grandma & Ryan ∼ I miss you. I wish you were here to see this.

To all the readers, reviewers, bloggers and authors, I thank you.

ABOUT THE AUTHOR

Heidi is a New York Times and USA Today Bestselling author.

Originally from the Pacific Northwest, she now lives in picturesque Vermont, with her husband and two daughters. Also renting space in their home is an over-hyper Beagle/Jack Russell, Buttercup and a Highland West/Mini Schnauzer, JiLL and her brother, Racicot.

When she's isn't writing one of the many stories planned for release, you'll find her sitting court-side during either daughter's basketball games.

Forever My Girl, is set to release in theaters on January 26, 2018, starring Alex Roe and Jessica Rothe.

Don't miss more books by Heidi McLaughlin! Sign up for her newsletter, follow her on Amazon, Book Bub or join the fun in her fan group!

Connect with Me!

www.heidimclaughlin.com
heidi@heidimclaughlin.com

ALSO BY HEIDI MCLAUGHLIN

THE BEAUMONT SERIES

Forever My Girl – Beaumont Series #1

My Everything – Beaumont Series #1.5

My Unexpected Forever – Beaumont Series #2

Finding My Forever – Beaumont Series #3

Finding My Way – Beaumont Series #4

12 Days of Forever – Beaumont Series #4.5

My Kind of Forever – Beaumont Series #5

Forever Our Boys - Beaumont Series #5.5

The Beaumont Boxed Set - #1

THE BEAUMONT SERIES: NEXT GENERATION

Holding Onto Forever

THE ARCHER BROTHERS

Here with Me

Choose Me

Save Me

LOST IN YOU SERIES

Lost in You

Lost in Us

THE BOYS OF SUMMER

Third Base

Home Run

Grand Slam

THE REALITY DUET

Blind Reality

Twisted Reality

SOCIETY X

Dark Room

Viewing Room

Play Room

STANDALONE NOVELS

Stripped Bare

Blow

Sexcation

The music sheet doesn't make any sense. I've been over it a hundred times or more and it's still all a blur. I know the lyrics and the beat, but everything I put down is a mess. Liam is expecting something from me by the time band practice starts in an hour, and I'm not going to be able to deliver. My mind is consumed with thoughts of love and lust and there isn't jack shit I can do about it.

I rip my ears buds out and move away from my computer. I can't do this, not today. Not after seeing her last night. I hate that I can't tell her how I feel. I hate that when another man looks at her, I feel nothing but murderous rage. I want to be the *only* one looking at her.

I'm a fool to think she wants me, with my full-sleeved tattoos and rocker lifestyle. I know I can offer her more than those other men. A stable home, financial security and a man who will worship and kiss the ground that she walks on. But I'm not the one you can take home to mom or to the school PTA meetings without being stared at. I know she doesn't want that. Enough people stare at her now.

I pull out a clean sheet of paper and write down more

lyrics. More touchy-feely shit that I wish I could tell her. Instead, I show up almost daily with something to offer her; coffee, lunch, or a free lawn mowing job because I can't, for the life of me, get it through my head that I'm nothing more than just a friend to her, and that's all I'll ever be.

I write down six words before tearing the paper up. I know why Liam tasked me with putting the music down for these songs, but they're mine. I hadn't planned on sharing them with the band. I think he's trying to get back at me for all those things I said about him falling in love when he returned home for his buddy's funeral. Now that it's my turn, he's sitting back and laughing his ass off. I ought to write some heavy shit. The head pounding scream-your-lungs-out shit that I sometimes think about. Either way, we need new songs and we've all been taxed with producing something.

But no, that isn't who we are. We've skyrocketed with Liam's heartfelt ballads and rocking personal stories that make women fall in love with us. They all think we're tortured souls and in need of companionship. Little do they know that Liam has only written about one woman. Hell, even I didn't know about it until he upped and left Los Angeles for the quiet, mundane life of Beaumont.

I can't blame him. I've done the same thing. This is the best place to raise Quinn. He'll go to school with Noah, and when Liam and I have a gig, Josie will take care of him. She's really filled the role of mother for Quinn and for that, I will forever be thankful to her. That and she gave my best friend a whole new life and we've since had a string of number one hits, putting us back at the top of the charts.

Now, if I could just get the one I'm infatuated with to just look in my direction. I'm firmly stuck in the friend category, though, and I don't know how to get out of it. I'm afraid to tell her how I feel because the look on her face will break me. I know she doesn't want me the way I want her, and I'd rather be her friend then not have her in my life at all.

I put my ear buds back in to try this one more time. I picture the things I want to do to her. The way I want to hold her. How I want to be the one she comes home to at night. Be the one that she turns to when she needs consoling on the anniversary of her husband's death. I want to be the one that the twins need when someone dares to break their hearts.

Imagining a life with her is as easy as breathing. I just have to find a way to make it happen without putting too much pressure on her. I hope that time is my friend and that someday she'll look in my direction and realize I'm someone she can trust to take care of her. That she'll know I'd never hurt her or the girls. That she will see me for me and know that Quinn and I would fit perfectly into her life.

I push away from the desk and head to my drums, bringing my laptop with me. I need to pound out some anger and frustration and maybe something will transpire that is usable. I close my eyes and let my sticks guide me. My beat starts off hard and steady. I'm beating the drums in front of me, releasing this pent up energy.

Her face flashes before my eyes, her voice inside my head. I instantly calm down and work out a rhythm. I hit record on my laptop and play the sound through. It's slow, smooth. Definitely something Liam and I can work on.

Jimmy and Tyler knock on the window, alerting me that they're here. Tyler is our new soundboard guru and he's been spending time with Jimmy in Los Angeles for the past week getting to know him. I stop the recording and take off my headphones to open the door for them. When I do, she's coming down the stairs talking on her cell phone. Her eyes meet mine briefly. I can't tell you if I'm smiling or not showing any emotion whatsoever, her presence alone makes me turn into a fool. It's times like this that I'm thankful she works for us. It gives me every conceivable excuse to be near her. It's so easy to fake a conversation about music and what gig we have coming up or what our deadlines are. The funny thing is, I know all of this, but act as if I've forgotten or can't find my phone to look it up.

Jimmy, or JD as we call him as he tells us it suits his 'rock star' lifestyle, slaps me on the shoulder as he passes. He's chuckling and muttering something to himself. Liam is trudging down the stairs before I can shut the door and turn on the light to let Katelyn and Josie know we are working.

I hate the way Liam looks in the morning. No, I shouldn't say that. I'm happy for him. He's with the one woman he loves and they are happy. Sickeningly happy; he's paid his dues and deserves this. The pride I see in his eyes when he looks at his son is the same way I am when I look at Quinn. They are the best of us, no matter how much we screw up.

"JD, my man," Liam says as they man hug. "I didn't hear you come in."

"Linda let me in. Tell me, how much did you have to pay her to leave her cushy job at the hotel to come here to take care of your sorry arse?"

Liam laughs. He made it a few months before he started looking for a housekeeper. He didn't want Josie having to take to care of the house by herself so he asked his former maid, Linda, to move to Beaumont. He's in the process of building her a nice little house behind his and he bought her a car.

"Let's get to work. Katelyn is working on booking some

new bars that she heard about, so we need to work out the kinks." Liam straps his guitar on and starts tuning.

"I worked this out before you guys got here." I move over the laptop and press play, watching JD and Liam as they listen to the melody. Liam smiles and looks over to the lyrics we've been working on. JD moves to the keyboard and hits a few keys and I add in the beat from my drums. Liam signals to Tyler to start recording. He strums his guitar and sings into the microphone as JD and I play along with him.

When I look up, Katelyn is watching me. Not us, but me, before she turns and is out of sight. For one brief moment I have a sliver of hope that she might feel the same way.